Bolan put the Uzi to work

To some small extent, Bolan would admit this was slightly personal. He had seen enough of Bowen's indiscriminate butchery in Brooklyn, where women and children were every bit fair game as their terrorist husbands and fathers, and the soldier wanted to be the man who bagged the traitor who did the dirty deeds for Phoenix Council.

And he'd lost Bowen once already. The man was still alive and kicking, murder his only game. There was no telling how many lives he'd snuffed out between New York and Chicago or how deeply involved he was in laying the foundation for wholesale slaughter.

This was duty, no more, no less.

The Executioner would get the job done.

MACK BOLAN ®
The Executioner

DON PENDLETON'S
THE EXECUTIONER®
FINAL STRIKE

THE
DOOMSDAY
TRILOGY
BOOK II

A GOLD EAGLE BOOK FROM
WORLDWIDE®

TORONTO • NEW YORK • LONDON
AMSTERDAM • PARIS • SYDNEY • HAMBURG
STOCKHOLM • ATHENS • TOKYO • MILAN
MADRID • WARSAW • BUDAPEST • AUCKLAND

First edition August 2002
ISBN 0-373-64285-7

Special thanks and acknowledgment to
Dan Schmidt for his contribution to this work.

FINAL STRIKE

Printed in U.S.A.

Strengthen your position; fight anything that comes.
—General W. T. Sherman

We must never forget the innocent lives that are lost to acts of terrorism. For them, I will make the men responsible pay for the pain they have caused and the lives they have destroyed.
—Mack Bolan

THE
MACK BOLAN®
LEGEND

Nothing less than a war could have fashioned the destiny of the man called Mack Bolan. Bolan earned the Executioner title in the jungle hell of Vietnam.

But this soldier also wore another name—Sergeant Mercy. He was so tagged because of the compassion he showed to wounded comrades-in-arms and Vietnamese civilians.

Mack Bolan's second tour of duty ended prematurely when he was given emergency leave to return home and bury his family, victims of the Mob. Then he declared a one-man war against the Mafia.

He confronted the Families head-on from coast to coast, and soon a hope of victory began to appear. But Bolan had broken society's every rule. That same society started gunning for this elusive warrior—to no avail.

So Bolan was offered amnesty to work within the system against terrorism. This time, as an employee of Uncle Sam, Bolan became Colonel John Phoenix. With a command center at Stony Man Farm in Virginia, he and his new allies—Able Team and Phoenix Force—waged relentless war on a new adversary: the KGB.

But when his one true love, April Rose, died at the hands of the Soviet terror machine, Bolan severed all ties with Establishment authority.

Now, after a lengthy lone-wolf struggle and much soul-searching, the Executioner has agreed to enter an "arm's-length" alliance with his government once more, reserving the right to pursue personal missions in his Everlasting War.

1

Bok Chongjin saw the specter of death. It was a face-less entity, cloaked in fire, that haunted his fears. Who-ever was hunting them like animals for slaughter caused him to sink fast to terror. He pondered the unbelievable spectacle of annihilation as they fled. The North Korean special-forces colonel took the warning light at skeletal face value, since paranoia alone inferred the original vision of conquest and glory was on the verge of dying a sudden, violent death. Yes, he thought, the dream had spiraled down to the point where all of them were staring over the edge of reality into the abyss of nightmare. A slew of questions ricocheted through his thoughts, when another voice of fear jolted him in his seat.

"Initiate Phoenix launch immediately... Yes, god-damn it, we will be heading directly for the airfield! Do not ask questions, Mr. Turner, understood? You are paid to obey! Repeat—initiate! Thank you!"

The launchpad for the dream or was it the beginning of the end? Chongjin wondered.

Angry with himself that his own faith was faltering, the colonel listened as his American counterpart, cofounder and chair of the Phoenix Council, barked further instructions to their subordinate at the main compound. The DIA pawn on the other end—one in a legion either in the loop or planted on the peripheral shadows of the great scheme—was obviously having considerable difficulty fathoming the dire urgency of their predicament. And who could blame him? Chongjin thought—even he was suspended in a state of horrified disbelieving animation.

The former Defense Intelligence Agency chief of countersurveillance, face flushed crimson and eyes bugged out, looked ready to ignite in spontaneous human combustion. Only Jeffrey Hill didn't go up in a supernatural ball of fire, but spittle flew, wild eyes mirrored the inner fears and the ex-chief's voice rose in new decibels of fury as he was forced to spell it out, step by step, talking to an idiot. Chongjin heard him snarl to start the roundup, Turner knowing already how to handle all those tagged as nonessential personnel. A check of the screen on the miniportable radar, Chongjin found it clear except for the routine air traffic from Tulsa and Oklahoma City.

"Have him raise Dragon's Head and see that it is manned until further orders are passed on," he told Hill.

While Hill ordered the antiaircraft battery to go operational, their own people on-site on Phoenix Red status, Chongjin leaned forward in his seat. He peered between the shoulders of his own operatives—the only two left standing after some human thunderbolt had razed their command center—and scouted the black skies, the vast darkness of the prairie. It might be fantasy bordering psychotic delusion, granted, but under the circumstances he imagined gunships winging down from the sky, with tanks and black-clad gunmen boiling up, the combined wraiths of doom bringing it all to a flaming, screeching halt even as all their countersurveillance and scanning probes showed no threat, air or ground.

But who among them, he wondered, could be certain of anything anymore?

Due south and coming up fast, he focused on the halogen lights. Some were built into the prefab domes, while other security eyes were mounted on narrow poles, staggered around the mile or more of perimeter. The spectral halo fanned across sweeping acreage, revealing armed shadows on the move to carry out the standing orders. The whole disjointed silver body of engineering and computational labs, the mammoth command and control central, and the recreation center—where the executions would take place—rose beyond the rolling tableland at this edge of the prairie.

Enough. The crisis was real; pull it together. A word in his own tongue to Wang Yik, and the shoulder holster with the 9 mm Browning Hi-Power pistol came from the glove box. He felt them watching him as he fastened himself into the holster rigging, checked the load on the pistol, chambered a round, then stowed the weapon.

Chongjin found it unusually hot and crowded in the van, the half-horseshoe surveillance console packing them together on narrow cushioned benches, but he attributed the heat and tight squeeze more to the sharp edges of their own shooting nerves than any lack of elbow room. He gave the three men a passing look in the flickering glow of the monitors. He wondered if one of them had simply given a stellar performance back at the war room, this trio minutes away from stripping off the masks to reveal the faces of wolves. Or was it one of the two FEMA men in the other vehicle who was the actor? Or both?

Soon enough he would see who was staying on board, or who had perhaps thrust a dagger between his shoulder blades. However it fell, from there on he would watch them carefully, keenly aware the first to bolt for the lifeboat would be revealed a traitor.

Chongjin found the NSA chief of counterterrorism peering through the convex portholes in the van's rear. The impulse to remind Mitchell Bernard the glass was bulletproof passed. The NSA man's eyes glittered against the firestorm, Chongjin assessing the look, wondering if it was a face of genuine fear and confusion or an act.

Who could say?

They were well out of range of missiles and streaking grenades, tracking bullets and whatever else. But the white fire of the incendiary blaze consuming the ranch house stabbed its light into the van's confines. As if, Chongjin concluded, the inferno's reaching glare were telling them they were next.

One man, Chongjin thought, and shook his head at the cause of all this horror and doubt. Who was this demon now on the verge of thrashing to oblivion the very thermodynamics of the council's brilliant shooting star, stomp their vision of a new world order through nuclear blackmail? Beyond the sheer unbelievable, it was insulting to him that they were chased, running like mongrels with tails between their legs and ahead of schedule, which alone compounded the dilemma. If it was what it appeared on the surface, well, this one-man wrecking crew had virtually walked up on the ranch house complex, a ghost in the night, driving grenades into the building, ripping out the guts of command center, shooting up the troops and nearly bringing the roof down on their heads. He could see the NSA honcho, the ex-DIA man and the present chief he'd passed the baton to ruminating, hashing over the debacle, trying, he suspected, to tally the odds. Between his own operatives and their trained so-called professionals, a rough guess and Chongjin put the dead and the dying back there at fifteen, twenty men tops.

Chongjin addressed them. "Listen to me. We must assume that since our adversary seized the element of shock, there will be no survivors back there. Focus on the next phase, gentlemen or we may find ourselves, like some of our late hired help, cremated. Speaking for myself, I didn't come this far to end up scattered in black ash across this barren land you call Oklahoma."

"Twenty-two shooters on the other end," Hill informed, as if he was trying to convince himself the numbers alone would be enough against this madman.

"One man," Bernard groused. "How? Who is he? What agency could he possibly represent?"

"I believe that was your department," Chongjin pointed out. The colonel felt his anger rising to a dangerous level. The others grumbled and scowled, wringing hands and popping knuckles.

"This will alter the schedule."

"You have a keen grasp of the obvious," Chongjin

told the acting DIA chief, letting the acid leak into his words.

Henry Jacklin, if Chongjin didn't know better, nearly sounded hysterical. "Has anybody here weighed the risk of capture once we hunker down in this ancient atomic fallout shelter in New Mexico?"

"Your point?" Chongjin said.

"It's impossible for us to simply call out there, what with all the scramblers and scanners, all the counter-surveillance interceptors. In other words, Colonel, we can't tell our guys to saddle up, show's on a little early, sorry, fellas, but we need to boogie. What I'm saying is that our window of escape, which was already narrow, is closing fast!"

Chongjin felt his gaze narrow. The DIA man was hugging the briefcase with all its vital data and access codes to various ballistic and technical data on the Medusa Project, jealously guarding the vaunted keys to the American Strategic Defense Initiative kingdom. Jacklin, of course, was referring, the colonel knew, to their ride from Nellis Air Range at 2400 hours that would fly in and scoop them up in New Mexico. The result of a last-minute contingency plan, a dangerous tinkering with the original formula, but...

"We stick to the new schedule. And it would appear we have been left no choice but to wait, Mr. Jacklin. I remind you all again, the area is controlled by our operatives, and should another unforeseen problem arise, I will be alerted in advance. One crisis at a time," Chongjin said, then ordered his driver to slow down, angle west toward the airfield, park it on arrival so he could assess the situation. "This trouble will pass, but only if we stay focused and united in our goal, and of course, let our people at the main compound do their job when this demon comes gunning for more trophies. Beyond your concerns, I must tell you I am very much displeased to state our counterintelligence is not all it should be."

The NSA guru wrinkled his nose. "We suspected the worst, Colonel, and it damn sure looks as if the worst is banging the brass knocker."

"I would say he is doing much more than that," Chongjin said.

Chongjin watched as the NSA man felt he was on the hot seat, appalled that he might somehow be viewed responsible for the catastrophe. "I believe it was discussed, Colonel, before the bombs began blowing down the house, that a black-ops team has rooted out our endeavor."

"A team? I saw no team. One man is all that appears to be barking at our heels," Chongjin said. "And need I say it appears he has plenty of bite."

There was a moment where they looked shamed by the truth. He could have gone on, picking their brains about the disaster in New York, where one of their three cells was eventually wiped out, thanks to a lone Iraqi fanatic who had jumped the gun and taken it upon himself to launch a personal jihad on a Manhattan subway. The colonel could have posed questions, framed with suspicion, about this superassassin of theirs, the Reaper. Such as how their killing marvel managed to escape the Brooklyn holocaust, unscathed, resituated in Chicago now, standing by for further orders. The cell there was already nervous, enraged about the fate of their comrades back east. If the situation report from Chicago was even remotely accurate, it sounded to him as if the terrorists were already banging on the gate to blow jihad throughout the city. Their assassin—whom Chongjin had never laid eyes on—had described the lone saboteur who had come blasting in on the execution team, botched their clean sweep of the Iraqi cannon fodder in Brooklyn, a hit ordered by Chongjin to both send a message to the other cells and to make sure they would not become property of American law enforcement. Well, Robert Bowen's vague description of this machine of destruction from New York matched the attacker who had choppered earlier to the main compound, fronting himself off as Special Agent Mike Belasko of the Justice Department.

It was time, Chongjin decided, to gauge reaction to his next proposal. "I suggest that all of us prepare to board once our flight from Nellis lands." An exchange of glances, their minds puzzling through exactly what that meant.

"I'm hearing another sudden change in plans, Colonel?" Hill asked. "You're saying the backbone of the council should pack a toothbrush and our classified laptops for the overseas trip? Leave it to subordinates and cronies on this end to watch our six, and make sure all the dominoes topple in order?"

Chongjin nodded. "Precisely." He let the weight of his silence settle. Bernard looked set to protest, but Hill and Jacklin appeared resigned to certain basic facts, common sense dictating new mission parameters. Somehow they had been discovered, a black-ops arm of the military perhaps now acting on suspicions generated, he fathomed, by the kidnapping angle involving the abduction of the project's four scientists who were on the cutting edge of the latest SDI technology. Perhaps loose tongues in the organization had aimed the guns their direction. Indeed, Chongjin knew there were weak links in the chain. Maybe one of their political stooges or a military puppet had grown a conscience. Thus it wasn't beyond the realm of duplicitous possibility someone had wriggled out of their iron grip, gone running to the FBI or the Justice Department to try to save their own small world. But these men were smart enough, Chongjin suspected, to realize they needed time and distance to sift through it all, let the smoke of this battle clear until they had concrete answers about their attacker or irrefutable evidence of any schemes that had been brewed behind their backs.

Jacklin nodded past Chongjin, indicating the SUV van running alongside them. "And our FEMA partners? Just like that, you think they'll skip the country in the interests of maintaining our agenda? All of us, one big happy family, phone home to our various agencies, extended vacation, back in two weeks?"

"They are men of reason, or so I hope. I believe they will see the logic to cut and run and seek a higher vantage point at this juncture," Chongjin said. "At least until we have answers. As for any concerns regarding suspicions cast their way from underlings, Department Of Defense, whoever, in a short time, it won't matter. We will have succeeded, victorious by the time some G-14 at DOD figures it out. Or...we will have failed. In that case our worries will be over, the dream dead."

Hill was nodding, weighing the matter with a grim

frown. "Okay, Colonel, with what's happened, and none of us is sure who is on to us or how much they know, I can see the wiser course for now is to put distance to CONUS."

Chongjin smiled. "And ride out this particular storm."

"I, for one, don't find the prospect," the NSA man said, "of lurching from one crisis to the next for some six thousand miles very attractive. Hardly discreet or promising the end results we seek. I hasten to point out when this blows up all the way back east, a shit-load of high-priority messages will be flying across every desk in Washington. Pentagon. Langley. Oval Office. And that's the short list. My own agency will wonder just where the hell I am, why I've disappeared off the face of the earth like the mother ship dropped out of the sky to take me away."

"I see I must remind you that you knew and accepted—or so you led me to believe—the risks inherent to the project before you came aboard," Chongjin said. "There are no gravy trains prepared to whisk us all to paradise, Mr. Bernard."

The NSA man pursued his argument. "Any number of satellites will be rerouted, Colonel, orbiting solely to zero in to shadow our flight once NORAD discovers there's a last-minute cancellation on their arrival board. We had planned to move ahead at roughly this time, yes, the whole nine yards of terrorist attacks, using them as extortion pieces if it came to that, or simply cutting them loose to keep Washington occupied until the flight cleared U.S. airspace. But I don't like having it all forced to go ahead so suddenly because of circumstances beyond our control."

"And do you have an alternative?" Chongjin posed.

"I'm afraid I don't. Looks like I have to go with whatever program is voted on."

"I am open to suggestions."

There were none.

They pondered in silence, their expressions darkening as the firestorm's glow faded with distance. Heads nodded, agreements grumbled.

Chongjin eased back in his seat. Hardly relaxed, he anticipated they hadn't yet seen the worse. They didn't know it, of course, but their consent, shaky as it was, had just saved their lives. With or without them, he would proceed on course to see North Korea transformed into a major nuclear superpower, with himself successor to the throne of Kim Jong Il. Carefully he read their expressions, suspected minds planning and plotting the future behind the eyes, seeing a future fraught with new peril. They knew where it went from there, once they put Oklahoma behind them, the road mapped out long ago. Now Chongjin found their faith crumbling at a time when they were called upon to lead from the front lines. Curious, he thought, what could be learned about others during crisis.

Bernard was the first to venture more concern. "According to my calculations, once we initiate phase two...need I spell it out? I'm referring to parachutes, our Pacific voyage. The plunge to the ocean, Colonel, the vanishing act."

Chongjin felt the return of the enigmatic smile he knew baffled or infuriated his American counterparts. "I have already factored that particular problem into the scheme."

"We allowed for forty parachutes," Bernard said. "The new math tells me somebody's going down with the ship."

"Then we will simply need to determine who is expendable when we reach that point."

There. He'd drawn the line in the sand, the bottom line; the dream itself was larger than the life of any one man in the council, no matter how high up the feeding chain. For now a veiled threat was enough, he decided.

There was still a madman on the loose to deal with, he feared. And Bok Chongjin hadn't come this far to see his ambition crushed by some loose black-ops cannon, one man or a thousand. If, he determined, there was betrayal among the group, if he didn't get what he wanted out of this joint venture, then no one would.

Everyone would die.

THE MILE-PLUS HIKE brought Mack Bolan to the northeast outer edge of open compound. The man known as the Executioner saw the frenzied activity near the airfield with men in black practically dragging occupants by the scruff of the neck out of mobile homes.

Bolan cut the pace, walking with purpose, M-16 sweeping the compass, and took a moment to gather his bearings.

Concrete intelligence usually provided the soldier with options, charted a course where he didn't get shot out of his boots off the starting line. Considering this was a classified military base, fenced in or not, where most of the who's who and what's what didn't even float in cyberspace, where they were a law unto themselves here, and the colossal odds against him had only begun to stack up. Even with the ultra covert Stony Man Farm's satellite imagery, able to zero in on a cowpie on the prairie, the Executioner didn't have much more than a ballpark tally on standing enemy numbers, much less precisely the lay of whatever mazes held the guts of the smattering of silver domes where shooters with hostages in tow could hunker down. He figured he'd already trimmed the enemy roster by fifteen, twenty shooters tops.

A roving head count of troops, and the soldier believed a full squad of hardmen, at the very least, was out of the hopper. The map-makers behind the lines, the strategy purists or brass with desks nailed to the seat of their pants would howl that the next stage of his assault was reckless, bordering suicidal or insane. Again, no options. Nothing short of a hard charge and a bayonet through the heart of the enemy, eye to eye, would win the night. And it wasn't the first time—but it could always be the last—where the house held all the marked cards and magnetic dice.

No fences barred any further penetration of the perimeter; no hardmen came running to intercept. Whatever the opposition's goal, shadows over the puzzle were getting swept away the deeper Bolan forged on into the campaign. What started as a subway massacre in New York, the kidnapping of an SDI scientist in the rolling, moneyed-up enclave of Middleburg, Virginia, had steered Bolan, step by bloody step, to this crossroads where the dark bottom line was just over the other side of the tracks.

A garbled cacophony of HK MP-5 subgun fire— sound suppressed or naked stuttering bursts—spelled out more of the enemy agenda. Hardmen, the Executioner saw, vectoring across a wide swatch of no-man's-land and securing temporary cover at the edge of a silver block, were torquing up the process of separating what they apparently considered wheat from chaff, grabbing shadows, barking orders, firing over their heads. The babble of shouting voices, the crying of children slashed the mix, but finally the angry hands-on corralling of the more resistant shadows from the tangled herd told the Executioner all he needed to know. Beyond whatever hostage shield already chosen, Bolan figured the murderous bastards had mass execution slated for any civilians that were viewed as expendable, those workers not on the enemy's A-list of SDI VIPs. Bolan knew the type. He'd seen it before.

And there were children, he saw, torn from the grasp of parents flailing and roaring their rage and horror.

Whether or not he was on the doorstep of revelation about the full agenda was moot. The cameras could track him; the gunmen could come blasting his way. The armed shadows bounding through the hatches of gunships, cranking over engines, had to wait.

The Executioner moved out, holding close to the silver facing of the first series of domed huts. Gunners were peeling away from the writhing mass of chaos, running for the command and control center, still tearing into mobile homes of Silver City, or shoving a couple dozen men, women and children toward the giant dome with its outdoor pool and tennis courts.

Bolan picked up speed, his combat senses feeling out the shadows.

There was no choice in his mind. The hardmen were

marching civilian prey for mass execution. The notion alone that they would slaughter children to cover and advance their own twisted agenda shot fire through the Executioner's blood. No way would Bolan proceed with any other avenue of attack when the blood of innocents was about to get spilled on his watch.

Not a chance in hell.

2

Adam Turner normally cut himself loose in the vault, free at last after all the day's stress and hassles. Dealing with classified humans, whether rocket-science geeks or black-ops thugs, wasn't easy work. Being the object of derision, when he wasn't outright ignored or shot up by snide remarks, took its toll, and on an ex-Marine, a bona fide war hero no less, with more medals than any amount of skeletons in his closet. Once upon a time, he thought, when there was pride and dignity to spare, if someone had talked down to him as if he were some bootlicking flunky...

That was then, and now, sad to the extreme, the old lion wandered the savanna, taunted by hyenas.

For instance, he thought, try asking one of the prima donnas to decode all the computational mathematic gibberish he was supposed to fax by way of update to DOD and he was treated to thinly veiled looks of scorn and disgust.

Despite the horror show about to grab center stage, live and in color on the monitors, he figured he had a few minutes left before last call. Considering all the crap he took just to keep the council's dirty secrets, make sure he had all their geeks in a row, he damn sure owed himself one more happy hour before the vault became just another piece of lurid nostalgia for the skeletons. As the boss who ostensibly ran the show out there, it was his right, his duty, to escape, he figured, to this playground of voyeur heaven, try to forget all the anger of the day he was made to swallow. Perks and privilege simply came with rank.

In keeping with routine, despite his darkening mood, the bottle of Jack Daniel's came out first. Down the hatch, a good medicinal jolt got the juices flowing. Easing back in the wheeled swivel chair, he scanned the monitors, waiting, hoping one of the younger wives— under fifty, at least, please and thank you, God—rolled up on the monitor, drew a bubble bath, shed the robe for the mini-cam disguised as the head of a screw in the bathroom's light fixture.

Each and every room in all of their double-wide trailers was watched and bugged, no exceptions, eyes and ears so tiny they blended in with the scenery. So he heard all the bitter or vile comments wives said about husbands to other women on base, and vice versa, pretty much the usual spousal hue and cry, lack of affection and sex, comments how hubby should maybe get a Viagra script. He knew their frustrations, dirty secrets, petty jealousies. He heard every argument, every last greasy shred of gossip. He saw every temper tantrum thrown by one of their little darlings, a few of whom sometimes caught an old-school shellacking— backhand to the chops, a belt to bared ass.

And naturally, knowing all the dirty tricks himself,

Armand Geller and black-ops company were exempt from having their own quarters on the second floor of the rec center under the microscope of Big Brother. And Geller, as far as Turner knew, was the only one besides himself who had full access to the vault's treasure chest. Personal code to the key pad, then there was fingerprint ID, voice box, retinal scan...

There was an outside chance, he realized, ghosts were hidden in the vault.

All things considered, it was going to break his heart to say goodbye to Big Brother. What man or woman, he thought, would want to give up the next-best thing to playing God?

The party was just about over, he saw, gunners breaching the outer perimeter of mobile homes, HK MP-5s fitted with sound suppressors, leading the charge. And just when Mrs. Burton, blond, all of thirty, an aerobics instructor, was set to drop the robe and ease into the tub. Then she stopped, clutching her robe, wheeling, startled, by the sound of a blacksuit knocking on their door.

And just like that, Turner turned to ice, dead inside. Normally, yes, another peep show, watching the monitors out of one eye to see if Geller was on the prowl, ready to burst in and deflate more than mood.

Well, if the monitors on the north end were any indication, the firestorm engulfing their precious command center, only two vehicles in working order and flying for the airfield, with Jeffrey Hill's voice rife with panic, full alert, antiaircraft battery raised from its bunker...

There was no escape, he thought. Not from the truth. Not ever.

And certainly not from what was about to happen.

It wasn't any one particular sordid event—the colonel's whores, the benders and blackouts, the shadows in the night with envelopes bulging with cash, toting blackmail pics in the other oily hand. All this, the trap sprung, just when two longtime buddies high up at DOD chose him as taskmaster for Project Medusa, which now left him wondering how many and how big were the gorillas hunkering on their shoulders.

And, no, it wasn't the veiled threats or the snubbing from the council. Those men, all of whom, just like himself, were traitors to their country, no more, no less. It was something deeper that stirred in his soul, a sleeping leviathan thrashing awake, demanding the pain to end, even if it devoured itself in self-evisceration.

He drank deep and long and watched the blacksuits going through doors, rounding them up, barking out demands. Beyond his rising fury, he felt himself about to float away in some out-of-body experience he was sure had to be induced by booze and regret. Gone, soon enough, he believed, would be all the anger, the self-pity and loathing, as the hot, simmering force at the core of his being crept closer to the surface.

Another swallow, just one more. And the cameras caught all the commotion and horror as hardmen barged in where technicians and scientists worked late out of their stations in Medusa Main. Turner looked away, hit the mute button for that one linkup as Big Brother's trained murderers began spraying civilians deemed nonessentials where they sat, banging away at keyboards. Or mowed them down eating dinner in the mess hall, or cut them to ribbons while lying in bunks, reading or sleeping.

With still more lives about to be snuffed out.

Then there were the children, God help them, he thought, some of whom weren't destined to make the trip with parents.

When first entering the vault, he had been far from honest with himself, but this *was* a different day, he knew. This was an hour of reckoning, as a stranger, a killing machine with righteous fire in his eyes, now walked among them. The guy, Special Agent Belasko, maybe had all the right credentials, to be sure, but Turner had seen something else in the man's eyes earlier in the day.

Judgment. And justice.

He had tried to lie to himself all would be well, but he could no longer deny Belasko knew the score there, and he was on the way to clean up the mess, take out the garbage.

Even as Turner saw their scheme unfolding as designed, the truck rolling in from the east end now with its hitched trailer of Chongjin's prize human cargo, Turner knew the party was crashed at the command center. Perhaps the revelation had stirred when the cameras detailed on close-up all the bodies of black ops laid waste to in about the time it took Belasko to stroll the grounds, shooting up the joint, blasting just about everybody to hell. One thrashing behind the man, but Turner suspected the stranger was only now getting it out of first gear.

He took another deep drink in search of a bliss he knew wouldn't come this night, no matter how soused. He fiddled a knob, adjusted the camera tracking north, and framed the armed shape charging from under the shadows hurled by the inferno. Turner chuckled, lifted the bottle in salute, when the guy—whoever he really was—spared a burst from his M-16 to blast the eye of that watching monitor.

A message, Turner knew, guy telling him he wasn't there for the guided tour or to talk reason.

So be it.

Turner trundled down the aisle. They were screaming in outrage and horror, kids wailing now. He glimpsed somebody in a white lab coat gunned down in a toilet stall, a maelstrom of more frantic pleas and questions washed away by long, stuttering fusillades of autofire. Another belt of whiskey, but he'd already decided only one of two options would take away the sick churning in his guts.

Turner dialed the combination lock and opened the drawer. What he was about to do was a far cry from some act of contrition, but compulsion to do something, other than sit there and watch the slaughter, to confirm he was little more than a traitor and a coward.

He took out the disk and a pen. It hadn't been all sordid fun and games there, he recalled, as the future revealed itself, one veiled look, one insult at a time. Redemption on the table maybe? Hardly. But there were secrets stored, what few details he could reveal about the council, their schemes, name, rank and serial number, so to speak, of the who's who, what's what. A safety net in the beginning, yes, but the sinking gut instinct clawed deeper each time he met with Chongjin. It was clear now, the more he thought about it, beyond his own foolish wants, he was expendable, every bit a nonessential, just strung along until they had the SDI mother lode.

He wrote the man's name on the disk, penned

Medusa, the access code that would allow entry into the files. He dropped it on the console. It was a long shot anything would come of it, that the guy would even make it down there to the vault, assuming he lived through the next few minutes.

The .44 Magnum Ruger Blackhawk was out of its holster, rising before he knew it. The finger curled around the trigger, then something froze his hand. Must be the last bit of good Catholic holding on, he figured as he stowed the gun. Hypocrite that he was, he hadn't seen the inside of a church in two decades, much less thought about any God. So, why now? Why bother? Fear, of course, was the obvious answer. He reckoned, too, pride—what little was left—weighed into the final decision.

One last drink, the bottle thudded down on the console. He was stalling, just the same, thinking no amount of booze could ever ease the constant ache always throbbing in his chest, wishing some alternate course could have saved him from the present. And no amount of the council's Judas silver would ever save him.

He saw two of Geller's boys bounding down the hall, hitting the steps for descent, coming for him. It didn't take the eyes of one of those Einsteins to see they were wondering why he wasn't responding to their calls, what the hell was he doing anyway while the rest of them were doing all the dirty work.

He stood and marched to the cabinet in the far corner of the cavern. There, he pulled out an HK MP-5, one clip fed to the subgun, a round chambered in place. Three spare magazines snug in his waistband, and he began heading for the steel door.

Call it one last self-serving act to somehow make it right, but Turner determined he wasn't about to keep eternity waiting on him much longer. The least he could do, he figured, was rake in a few markers.

"YOU PEOPLE FUCKED with the wrong Marine, son!"

Turner chuckled at Walton, one of Geller's boys who was always concerned about the well-being of the wives on base, crawling now for his subgun, one hand trying to hold in his guts. Big stud now, Turner thought as he let loose rumbling laughter, making sure he grabbed the guy's full attention. The sight of this slug leaking blood all over the floor, stone-cold confusion and terror in his eyes, sent Turner soaring to some plane of righteous anger-driven ecstasy, it seemed, watching himself outside his body.

A goddamn avenging angel.

He was alive, all right, he was back, the old Marine war hero, the lion on the prowl, taking no crap, kicking ass. The way it should it be. Never a doubt.

Turner kept on chuckling, taking his time, a few slow paces down the narrow corridor that would eventually take him outside to carry on. He couldn't help himself suddenly, indulging the moment to visualize four—soon to be five—kills. Two ops heaped in the vault's doorway, shot to shit, the realization, too late, that somebody had misjudged old Adam Turner, the punching bag for everybody's silent condescension and smart-ass uppercuts. These three, same deal, coming to round him up. Catching them in midflight, dropping them, one, two, three.

Got to be strong, got to be strong, he heard his mind laughing at him in some singsong way.

"Looks to me you need the number for that bus just run you over, son," Turner said, allowing Walton to drop a bloody hand over his subgun, then stitched a burst of subgun fire up the man's back.

And that made five. Crucified, and on the way to hell.

He heard the tac radio crackling with Chongjin's voice next, and plucked it off Walton's belt. The whole din of chaos burst out the radio as he punched on, Chongjin shouting questions.

"Yes, Colonel?"

"Where are you?"

The chuckle came out as a strange giggle in his ears. "I'm on the way, Colonel."

"What is wrong with you? We need every available hand!"

"Fear not."

"What are you babbling about!?"

Turner tossed the handheld away, Chongjin's angry shout diminishing to bleating curses. The same floating feeling took him to the door. Outside Turner weighed the problems and the pandemonium. It could have been some calamity, he thought, supernatural or otherwise, straight out of the Bible. All these murderers and thieves, he judged, all the lying and deceiving civilian congregation about to be punished for sex sins. Wailing and gnashing of teeth, it was, Sodom and Gomorrah about to be vaporized off the face of the earth by the wrath of God. Treachery, perhaps the cousin to anger, Cain and Abel, but on some epic scale.

So what was he? Turner wondered, moving for the gunships. The prodigal son, waking up to the folly of his evil ways, burned out by grotesque self-indulgence? Judas? Shamed to despair, lurching on now for the hanging tree, the blood silver falling from his hand? And the council? Washing their hands of all this death and horror, handing over women and children, lambs for the slaughter? Maybe the meek, he thought, wouldn't inherit the earth, or at least not until the strong took everything they wanted.

The subgun felt a little light in his grip. Aware he'd gotten carried away out of the gate, Turner fed the MP-5 a fresh clip for the final leg of the journey.

One death. One chance to make it right.

3

Bolan navigated the maze of domes and squat blocks, mindful of mounted cameras, alert for the appearance of hardmen.

Almost there. Closing hard on the enemy, scouting for the next available cover, the soldier knew his options were down to zero, no choice but to start tagging the opposition with the M-16.

Out on the airfield, the terror edged toward hysteria, the hole in the dam of panic cracking. The Executioner heard men demanding answers, the smaller children crying louder, the group tugged and prodded along by as many as ten troopers. Which left how many in the gunships or prowling the compound? Three groups appeared broken up to Bolan, for one reason or another, a staggered herd as black-clad hardmen maintained a loose phalanx, ushering the civilians with menacing words and wagging subguns, any stragglers shoved and barked at to keep moving. The ruse, it sounded, was for the men to inform, in the sort of shouting and swearing that would have made an old-school Marine DI proud, that the base was under attack, as if that was meant to answer all questions and calm nerves.

How right they were, Bolan thought. He knew he had one hope to turn the tide. These men were the worst kind of savages to Bolan, traitors who would murder anyone in their way, even a small child, to steal cutting-edge technology, along with their abducted SDI creators. To top it off, there was the potential holocaust of more terrorist attacks in the hopper.

Crouching at the southwest edge of the command building, Bolan flicked the selector switch to single-shot mode. He lifted the M-16, sighting on the closest gunner, the hardman whirling around as if he sensed some unseen danger. So far, the general chaos had covered the soldier's advance, but he knew the troops were alerted, edgy and trigger-happy.

Bolan was seconds away from letting the enemy know he was back in play. It was a dicey proposition, going for a few quick clean kills, working his way next for the cover of the motor pool, hoping a few of the hardier souls would see the one opening to make their dash for freedom, and help galvanize the others into a stampede for some pell-mell exodus.

An isolated scene erupted just beyond the motor pool. A civilian was flapping his arms, grabbing at a gunner, explaining himself. Bolan caught the gist of the hue and cry, something about how the man didn't belong there, it was all a mistake. From the black gunships, the soldier spotted two more men charging out of the rotor wash, shouting a name—Blankenship, Bolan believed.

Misery yet to spread around, plenty of oversight and miscalculation that night already on the part of the opposition. Bolan factored the enemy's supreme arrogance was keeping him in the game, unaware he was on the premises.

Their mistake, and their problem.

One last search of the way he'd come—all clear—
and Bolan took up slack on the trigger.

CHRISTOPHER BLANKENSHIP felt the panic welling toward hysteria the farther he was force-marched beyond the gunships. Heading toward the recreation center with the other civilians—technicians, mathematicians, laborers and families—all of them were clueless about what was actually happening and why. Worse, making it all the more unbearable and frightening, his wife was right beside him, screaming questions at everybody within earshot and yards beyond. But he ignored her, as usual, demanding for once to be heard himself. As anticipated, she directed her next barrage at him, the salvo divvied up with vile cursing, the usual live grenades about his manhood—or lack thereof—going off in his face, then one nuke she'd clearly been holding on to launched at this crunch time from the reserve silo. Oh, God, how he despised her, her very existence a blight on the planet Earth—all the henpecking, constant demands for affection, the vicious digs when he was too damn tired or simply uninterested in her mating calls after one of her hour-long drunken tirades—but this was no time to reminisce how much his third and her fifth marriage sucked.

The guards, the ones who counted the most, weren't listening to him! Morons! Even if they did live in some sordid world of guns and murder, so far beneath the cerebral cosmos he inhabited they weren't even ants on the ground, he wasn't about to cut them slack for sheer stupidity, not at a time like this. If they didn't see their oversight, whatever. The choppers would lift off, leaving him stranded.

Compounding the horror, he'd already seen the trio led at gunpoint into one of the choppers, hauled from the trailer hitched to the semi. The black hoods threw him for a loop, but that would be none other than Thomas Shaw, the elder genius of the SDI quartet, his family in tow. Months back, he had talked to Shaw during a trip to D.C., hinting changes could be on the way, planting the seeds for this moment when they might consider their collective future, bigger offers than the table scraps DOD could possibly bestow upon them. Typical Shaw—nose to the grindstone, don't rock the boat—his response they were the future of SDI, and he was quite content with life as it was. Well, the future had arrived, and Blankenship, because of some flunky's ignorance of who and what he was, couldn't allow the gravy train to pull out of the depot without him.

That was tantamount to suicide.

It wasn't supposed to be this way, he heard his mind cry. The man named Geller had vowed he'd be taken from the base with the others who were chosen to build a future SDI program for some undetermined foreign benefactors, details unclear. It was about the money first, of course, prestige second but hardly last, all the trimmings of fame and fortune he'd so far been denied, his colleagues always seeming to steal his thunder, grabbing the spotlight on cable talk shows, snapping up the six-figure book deals. Why would he take the man's money anyway, pass on bits and pieces of classified material the whole time he was there, if he wasn't prepared to go the distance with these people? Why would he bother to look into the future, the promise of reward beyond monetary for his brilliance paving his own golden road toward the distant horizon where glory waited? What the hell was going on here?

He reached out, took the black-clad security guard by the shoulder, shaking him in a dangerous moment, realizing the spook could go either way. "Listen to me! I'm Christopher Blankenship! I'm one of the Titan Four! I belong back in that helicopter! There's a mistake! I'm supposed to be leaving with your people—your boss! Check it!"

He saw the tough-guy veneer—why did these spooks all look alike, same buzz cuts and chiseled razor features, with beady eyes peering at him? The shouting and wailing seemed to fade, as he felt hope flicker, the guy thinking that maybe there was a mistake.

"Yeah, that's right, I know you've heard my name!"

"Chris? What's happening? What are you saying? You're talking crazy, you're going to leave me here? Answer me, don't just stand there like some wimp!"

Damn right he was leaving her, he wanted to say, but instead he threw Sandy his best sympathetic face, hoping she backed off once she saw he was cowed by her once again, and said, "It's going to be all right, honey. Just do as they say. I'll work this out. And, please, try to calm down. You're not doing yourself or anybody else one iota of good with this hysterical outburst."

But how could he be sure about anything, especially with his own immediate future uncertain, none of these morons with guns seeming to know how important he was?

"Don't patronize me, you asshole! Something's wrong here, do something, be a man for once..."

And so on and so forth, Blankenship turning a deaf ear to the demonic mantra he'd heard a thousand times, praying those two men charging from the gunships were coming to save him.

"Blankenship!"

There it was! Someone calling his name. Someone with far more clout than these simpleminded baboons had realized the gross mistake. Understandable, with all the chaos and confusion, of course. Kids were crying for their mothers and there was a raging fire in the distance where he believed the spooks housed most of their classified countersurveillance, or whatever really went on there. And what was the problem that way all about? Something to do—

Forget about it. He was out of there.

"Here! Right here!"

Blankenship saw one of the two spooks, thank God, checking his face against the photo ID, head nodding in recognition.

"You're some special character we've got to come hunting for! Shag your ass!"

No problem, he was already wrenching free from Sandy's claw on his arm, her poisonous invectives lashing his back. Again, no sweat, free at last, clearing the prison bars, checking out. There would always be another bimbo—he'd have his choice once the bank account swelled and the world finally realized and paid due homage to the up-and-coming star of the Titan Four. On his way now, head bent to bull into the pounding rotor wash when—

He heard the shooting first, the cries of pain next, then he realized he was alone, the spooks spinning like tops, falling. What the hell? He felt his bowels rumbling to cut loose, aware that blood was smacking him in the face, realizing, too, the spooks were dead before they hit the ground. Jolted by new terror, he ran for the gunship, unfamiliar faces in the doorway, two or three spooks with weapons blazing at somebody, subguns scissoring in different directions, as if they didn't know whom to shoot at or where. He was terrified they meant to gun him down, then he was hollering his name, getting attention, a hand reaching down, hauling him up. Bullets were now snapping like crazed hornets as he barged into the gunship, faces a blur, his chest heaving. Someone was roaring, "Lift off!" And he was doing his damnedest to wedge a path through the spooks, seeking any haven from the bullets that were whining off metal. He wasn't sure what made him freeze, a grip of relief or the look on Thomas Shaw's face. It wasn't much longer than a split second, but he felt the elder Titan's stare, knowing, judging, penetrating.

Reading him, loud and clear.

Blankenship was lifting a leg, sifting through any number of reasons and justifications, when he felt the bullets tear up his back, flinging him down into blackness.

THE NIGHT CLEARLY belonged to chaos, death and treachery. With the good and the bad on the doomsday clock, the Executioner's first three shots had to be on the money.

They were.

Two swift tags, cored through the face by a 5.56 mm

round each, and the lagging herd froze for a moment before it must have hit them it was way beyond repair, or some form of cavalry had ridden in for the rescue. Civilians started grabbing each other, husbands or co-workers perhaps slinging women to the ground, mothers shielding children. As hoped for, enough non-combatants hit the deck, out of the line of fire, when Bolan caressed the trigger and waxed the shooter who was swinging the MP-5 his way off his feet. A few errant rounds sailing for the sky, but Bolan had delivered another clean head shot, shaving down the odds. Three heartbeats, three pulls of the trigger.

The fuel of more mayhem, though, was dumped into the fire. Gunmen took the siege, bulling more angry steam into the pack of civilians in mobs, winging sub-gun fire over their heads, hollering for them to run toward the chain-link fence.

A runner had bolted from pack three. Whoever he was, Bolan smelled a rat either way, but the guy was already yanked through the hatch of a gunship, with his wife or lover, Bolan presumed, cursing her abandonment. An unknown shooter then snared a second of Bolan's attention, as the two hardmen who'd come calling on pack three were dropping near the pylon of the gunship. The hatch was filled with sparks and ricochets next, as gunners stood in the doorway returning subgun fire, spraying the tarmac and the motor pool. One of the men sponged up bullets from an undetermined shooter, jigging in the hatch, then taking a header to the tarmac. Aware the night's big catch was wriggling out of his net, the Executioner cursed as the gunships lifted off.

Too much to do, no time.

Homing in on the racket of the mystery guest, and Bolan made out the beefy silhouette. A cowboy. Rolling on, a weird grin on his face, shouting something unintelligible as the man kept pounding the hatch with his SMG, raking his own gunmen with extended bursts. Whether it was guilty voices in his head or whatever plunged the man over the edge of sanity, Bolan would never know. The second hardman toppled out of the hatch, crunching up on the helipad but not before he nailed the cowboy. The dark spray flying from the man's head, the guy dropping in a boneless sprawl, and Bolan knew he could forget any field grilling.

It was going to hell on all points. Gunships up and flying, and Bolan noted they were headed on a southwest vector. A body tumbled out the hatch, but Bolan didn't have a second to waste being bogged down with speculation and anxiety. He was focused on the living, namely the innocent. He saw the battery of SAMs, a dozen warheads pointed up, unmanned, but unseen hands could cut loose the works with an electronic touch. Small blessing he couldn't raise his own blacksuits from Stony Man Farm. The Kiowa wouldn't stand a chance against that firepower.

No cover to cut the distance to the hardmen forcing the civilian through the gate now, so Bolan hoped a little luck would come his way with another SUV battering ram. The first vehicle showed keys in the ignition. He was opening the door, his senses assaulted by the human din, when four gunners rounded the northwest corner, shadow blurs, but going for it. The M-16/M-203 combo was up, chugging out a 40 mm payload, Bolan watching the grenade wobbling on.

The blast erupted in the heart of the quartet, every hardman soaking up shrapnel and fire.

Down. How many more?

Two civilians were rising, hauling in discarded weapons. At this stage, blind panic had set in, and the soldier knew he was as fair game as any of his enemies unless he made them see reason.

"Justice Department!" Bolan announced, directing it toward the duo who acted as if they knew how to use the weapons. "Get these people into one of those mobile units and wait for me."

"What the hell is going on here?"

They hesitated, but Bolan didn't have the time to squabble. "You want to make it through the night, get it in gear and clear out! I'm here to help. End of story."

He left them to it, hoping no more gunmen charged the airfield to cut them down.

Bolan was in the SUV, cranking it up, flicking the M-16 to full-auto fire. Another 40 mm frag bomb ready in the M-203, the Executioner dropped it into drive and whipped the vehicle away from the motor pool.

The men were ready this time, pros who knew it was going the full distance.

Not even a dozen or so yards and bearing down on the rec center, and Bolan saw his targets shuffle ahead, then cut loose with subgun fire.

4

Unlike what he'd heard, the truth didn't set Thomas Shaw free. The truth—or some of it—wanted to reveal itself as a shout in the night, followed by the briefest look into the eyes of the betrayer. Both were familiar, and confirmed suspicion of conspiracy.

There was no time now, however, to dwell on the swelling enormity of their predicament, all the various human—or inhuman—factors, or ponder questions darting through his mind about Christopher Blankenship. The youngest of the Titan Four was dead, shot up by unknown gunmen after he rushed into the chopper, crying out in a voice Shaw imagined belonged to passengers terrified of being stranded on the *Titanic*. It was sickening, on top of all the other horror, to hear the terrified, near childlike pitch in his colleague's voice. The man was only concerned that he might be left behind, save him first and last, to hell with everybody else. Whoever had purchased his allegiance, though, didn't seem bothered by his death, as Shaw heard the Korean in the cashmere coat order the removal of Blankenship's body. Shaw wasn't one hundred percent certain his colleague was dead, but his body was dragged across the floor, trailing a puddle of blood, limbs twitching, and tossed out of the helicopter by one of the armed black-clad operatives with all the concern of someone throwing away garbage. No matter how callous the act, the message was clear. They were all expendable; any wounded individual was a burden to be quickly shed.

Shaw knew he couldn't say what all the shooting at the classified SDI compound was actually about as the chopper gained altitude and speed, leaving the mayhem behind to run its course. Whatever the human equation behind the war zone, it nonetheless struck a chord of hope in Shaw. Someone knew what was happening there, and now sought to charge to their rescue. Silently he wished the unknown attackers good luck and God-speed, their captors the worst possible misfortune.

The four strangers up front were engaged in an argument, the chaos or cause of it obviously unnerving them. The anger and fear on their faces was a near perfect match for what Shaw found on the mob of abductees. He checked on his wife and daughter, heart sinking, gut clenched with sickness as he read the terror, aware there was nothing he could do except tell them to hold on, hope, offer whatever comfort and words of assurance he could. He was a scientist, not a warrior who could stand up and challenge men of violence, but something inside was waking up, rising by degrees with each leg of the journey. It was primal and dark, a fearsome boil to strike back, but he chose to shove it to the black hole where desire was more fantasy than any plausible course for retaliation. Seeing they were safe so far, just being there, was strange relief now that the hoods were gone and they were able to see each other. Together, but for how long? What was next? And where was his other daughter? Was Sara safe? Did the FBI, Justice Department have her under their protective umbrella?

All he could do, he realized, was pray and hope.

Somehow the three of them had made it into the back of the fuselage, claimed one of the benches while the others, perhaps twenty bodies in all, were squeezed around them, taking up whatever space they could find, standing or sitting. Thankfully the three of them hadn't been split up during the commotion.

They were together for the moment, with no choice but to ride out whatever was happening. And there was no point drumming up any one of a dozen worst-case scenarios, where they were going or why. Fear could break a man when someone else most needed him to remain calm and strong.

Shaw smiled at Rebecca, dropped his bound hands over hers and squeezed.

"Thomas?"

"We'll be fine," he told his wife, his voice muted by the whirl of anxious voices demanding their questions be answered. Turning to his daughter, he said, "Patti." It was odd, again, bordering obscene, he briefly thought, how something so simple—seeing the faces of his family—could feel such a blessing. "Stay strong. I won't let you or your mother out of my sight."

"People! Listen to me very carefully!"

The Korean edged toward the abductees, scanning the crowd, addressing them in a voice of authority and demand, the angry dictator, Shaw thought. He wondered who the Korean was, but before the line of questions took shape a voice from the crowd began barking.

"Who are you? You care to tell us what is going on here? I guess we have Korean spies now looking to steal classified technology, is that it? I suppose you're going to stand there and tell us we're not victims of a mass kidnapping?"

Shaw didn't recognize the demanding one, but why would he? Out of these gathered hostages, he had only worked personally with Jason Monroe, Dwight Parker and, of course, the late Chris Blankenship, but never in Oklahoma. The two remaining Titan Four scientists were wedged into the crowd, their wives holding on to them. If they were traitors, as he had expected Blankenship had been, he couldn't discern any guilt or shame on their expressions. At the moment, he couldn't be sure of what he knew, much less whom to trust beyond his own blood.

"Very well, I am North Korean, to be precise. Mr...?"

"We'll skip the friendly preamble, okay. I want to know how you think—"

"As you wish."

Before the man could launch into another round of demanding questions, the Korean reached into his coat, withdrew a pistol and shot him in the face. A paralyzing moment of shock, gasps and feeble-sounding curses hit the air, then the Korean growled at the gunner to dispose of the body. Point made, Shaw knew, sick to his stomach, but managed to turn to his wife and daughter, then softly shook his head, hoping there was enough stern warning in his eyes, telling them to keep still and quiet.

"Enough! No questions, and there will be no crying! Silence, whore!" he roared, as a woman's sobs sounded from the deep shadows, the fuselage door flung back, the latest corpse thrown out into the night. "Now, I apologize to all of you for that individual's misunderstanding. He was so smart, he couldn't save himself. Your IQs will save none of you should you question my authority."

Shaw felt his stomach churning as the realization sunk in that they were all staring into the eyes of insanity.

"There are primary individuals among you, and there are secondary workers. Some are more valuable to me than the rest," the Korean said, and Shaw felt his narrowed gaze wandering his direction. "You will do as you are instructed. You will go where you are told to go. Should you even hesitate to obey, secondary individuals will be singled out for punishment. That will be all for now. If there are no further outbursts..."

Shaw watched, felt the horror growing around him as the man bared a strange smile, enjoying some private joke. He corrected his original assessment of the North Korean. What he found smiling in the shadowy light was the face of pure evil.

"Enjoy the rest of your flight."

THE HARDMAN MADE a fatal mistake when he let his human shield move on. He was wide open, just on the other side of the open gate in the chain-link fence, when the Executioner hit the M-16's trigger, tagged him with a burst to the chest and sent him flying, arms windmilling before he splashed down into the pool.

The SUV rolled on, cut back to ten miles per hour before the soldier bailed. Bolan advanced, covered on the starboard side, ready to charge through the gate, M-16 tracking for live ones.

He didn't have to wait long. More subgun fire opened up again as three backpedaling hardmen were heading for an open hatch on the far side of the pool. They were framed for several heartbeats in the soft bands of halogen lights, jostling civilians and cursing. Their second barrage slashed the SUV again, the vehicle already brutalized by the first rounds, slugs hammering the grille, peppering the windshield with spiderweb designs before glass exploded. The soldier slit his eyelids against the hurricane.

As the fence absorbed the SUV's charge with a groan of bending metal, Bolan was breaking cover, through the gate as the gunners melted inside the hatch. One hardman popped out, milking a short burst of SMG fire as the Executioner bolted down the deck, slugs shrieking off concrete. Bolan was past the diving board when his adversary vanished into the hatch. Now what? Something about the shooter's sudden vanishing act didn't feel right to Bolan. Well, there was no other way Bolan could see, the entire domed structure apparently made of one giant slab of silver alloy. Figure three, maybe four shooters left, the clock already wound down, and he wasn't going in to take any prisoners. He needed them nailed and out of play, the civilians rounded up, a thorough walk-through...

Getting ahead of himself.

The mixture of angry and terrified voices came hurtling out of the hatch, an echo chamber that warned

Bolan some narrow corridor waited. He hit the edge of the hatch and crouched as the wave of voices faded. Every fiber of combat instinct tuned to whatever lay dead ahead. He sensed a presence lurking at the far end of the corridor.

Bolan surged in, already taking up slack on the M-16's trigger, and his gut instinct rewarded him with the edge to get the drop on the man rolling around the corner. The hardman's SMG started to blaze, but Bolan was nailing him with a full-auto barrage of man-eaters, crotch to throat, the 5.56 mm hammer driving him back in a spasming jitterbug before he sailed off his feet.

Two voices, if he judged them right, snarled out demands and threats, just around the far corner. The Executioner ran on, made the edge of the corner, a wide lobby fanning out from his cover, when he heard, "Hey, whoever you are, toss out the weapon or we start killing these civilians! You hear me? There are women and kids here! You want to be a hero, come on, then! Show yourself! I know you're there!"

To his left, Bolan determined, maybe twenty, thirty feet away. He thumbed the selector switch for single shot, drew a deep breath, let the limbs loosen and walked out into the open.

"You don't listen so good, pal! Drop the goddamn weapon!"

Maybe they had reached a breaking point, holding down their terror, primal instinct telling them they were marched in there to be executed but enough bodies in the mob broke, scrambling in different directions to give Bolan all the room he needed to nail it down. Two shooters, one on each flank, and Bolan dropped the man who had swung his SMG toward the runners. The guy was kicked off his feet, a dark hole blossoming between his eyes, when the Executioner waxed number two with a second head shot.

Bolan announced himself, singled out two men who looked capable of restoring some calm. "Get everybody outside."

"You say you're with the Justice Department?" one of his volunteers asked, doubtful.

"You want a résumé?" The Executioner searched the banks of double doors that led to what he assumed were game rooms, perhaps an auditorium. "Any more of these goons on the loose?"

"You got the last of them, or at least the ones in here."

Bolan intended to check every foot of every last building just the same. He was far from done. A lengthy search, and he might turn up some answers about the enemy who had flown on, a clue about their destination and scheme.

"You know," the man said, some of the hardness melting off his features as he glanced at the corpses, the women and children being gathered in by Bolan's other volunteer, "what I'm thinking they herded us in here for?" A pause, the guy peering at Bolan, nodding to himself. "You know, don't you?"

"Whatever it was, they can't do it now."

"YOU'RE RESPONSIBLE for the whore. Take care of it."

Robert Bowen, aka the Reaper, was building another whiskey by the wet bar, dumping in two cubes, when the North Korean made his demand. It was bad enough, he thought, the shadow was shadowed, the baby-sitting was baby-sat. Now they were telling him to lose the call girl, when he figured he hadn't quite squeezed his six hundred bucks' worth of fun and games out of her yet. One pop only for his money, the blonde waiting in the bedroom for round two, bought for the duration. And he was being told to call it a night, down to business, they didn't have time or concern for a man's simple pleasures. March into the bedroom, they wanted, shoot her now since she had seen their faces. No problem. Well, he had problems, all right, he figured, but he was about to have two less worries in a few moments.

The two headaches in question were sitting, smug and inscrutable, on the couch, the North Koreans packing pistols beneath their jackets, one set of eyes watching him, the other staring at CNN. And this, he thought, was the council's idea of mutual cooperation between their respective countries? One side calling all the shots, ready to go on the muscle if orders weren't obeyed at the snap of fingers. It didn't work that way for Bowen. No way in hell, not when he was the one whose butt was on the firing line, taking all the risks, doing the bulk of the killing.

Supposedly, Bowen thought, he was in Chicago, holing in a suite at the Sheraton Chicago Hotel and Towers, complete with scenic view of the river, to monitor their Iraqi situation. In other words, the terror imports weren't supposed to jump off the starting block as one of their own had in the New York subway massacre, kicking off an escalating mess that threatened the Phoenix Council with exposure. The Iraqis were to wait for the all-important call from up top, no matter how antsy they were to initiate jihad in the Chicago streets. Or so Turner told him to tell them.

Hold their hands in the meantime.

A lot had gone wrong, disastrous, in fact, since New York. He had lost an entire crew of shooters, two of them shot by his own hand after he'd bailed to leave the others to do the dying, using them to cover his escape. It might have worked out differently—not a single casualty on his team—but for the big nameless stranger, a ballsy X factor storming in on his backside when they'd hit Brooklyn to close down the Iraqi shop there. The guy chopped down his men as if they were rookies who'd never heard a shot fired in anger. It was a miracle of sorts, combining guile and cunning naturally, that Bowen had even made it out of New York to Chicago. Just one more point of confinement now, doing what he was told to do, when and how. Sure, it was their suite, their money and guns, but Bowen never let anyone other than himself run the show. All that, but he just plain didn't like their attitude.

And he was still haunted by the commando, which was perhaps the single biggest reason he would stick with the program, ride it out in Chicago, even solo, then see what his order of business was in Los Angeles. According to Turner, the man must be Special Agent Mike Belasko from the Justice Department. With any luck, once the fireworks began going off in Chicago, this Belasko would show up, drawn to the bloodletting like a shark to chum. Or one could always live in hope, he decided. Bowen didn't think he could live with himself if he didn't get one more crack at the guy.

He figured he was owed, and more than just money.

So far, despite the sudden arrival of the two North Koreans, Chicago was shaping up as promised by his DIA contact, Adam Turner. The U-Store-It, part of a chain of storage warehouses owned and operated by Korean lackeys in the three targeted cities, had turned up his latest weapons, predetermined coded instructions and walking-around cash. It was good to be armed again, itchy for action, even if he was looking to redeem himself in his eyes after New York, and he didn't care if it hit the fan in two minutes or two hours. Sooner was better, since the biggest pain in the ass right then was the fact he didn't care much for the North Koreans turning up when he was running their errands around town, insisting they keep him company, holding him the whole time in thinly veiled scorn, as if they didn't trust him to do his job.

Which was never clearly defined, other than paying a few of the Iraqis a face-to-face once he hit Chicago, warning them to hold on for the phone to ring. Other than making sure they got from point A to B, his role was vague at best. Then, of course, there was the possibility the North Koreans were on hand to tidy up one Reaper as the final loose piece of business. If it was viewed in that light, he knew it was always best to clean up potential messes as he went along before they turned lethal.

"At your earliest convenience, Mr. Bowen. If you don't mind."

Oh, these guys were beautiful, he thought, sipping his drink, taking his time. They had all the answers, talking down to him in that tone. What they couldn't possibly know—unless he told them—was that he was privy to some of the more critical details of their big play, thanks to Turner and Geller out in Oklahoma, guys he'd done a few dirty deeds for in the past. The North Korean faction of the council had essentially been sought out, groomed by rogue elements in several U.S. intelligence agencies. FEMA types were somehow dumped in the mix, part of the coming master plan to declare martial law once the council's doomsday army—stationed and waiting on some remote Pacific island—descended on American city streets, armed with nerve gas, backpack nukes, the works to take and hold down a major U.S. city. That was at some point in the future, though, once certain political flunkies and high-ranking military brass were positioned in the wings of high power close to the reins, as in Oval Office and the Pentagon. The immediate plan was to bag four top rocket scientists to advance the North Korean missile program along with a various assortment of SDI brains and conceptualizers, state-of-the-art ballistics folks. Then commandeer a prototype spy plane from Nellis Air Range. All aboard in Oklahoma, once the nonessential personnel was dealt with, then use their hostages as leverage to make sure they safely cleared American airspace. Meanwhile, unleash an army of Iraqi fanatics, since the country's leader was promised delivery by the council of missiles, guidance systems and other techno goodies to put his country back on the map and, in the same breath, let the leader get even for all the tonnage of bombs dropped on his head. One big happy family.

On the surface, Bowen thought it appeared a mad

scheme, doomed to suicide, too much action spread around too thin, too quickly, but so far the pieces were falling into place. The only drawback to conspiracy, though, he knew from experience, was that one domino toppling, the one link in the chain severed, and then everything else went to hell. If one guy started squawking, pointing fingers to save himself then the only thing left was to hear the fat lady sing.

He took the Browning Hi-Power pistol from the nylon bag at the base of the wet bar, threaded the sounded suppressor to the customized fit.

"Let me tell you two something. You're far from the smartest guys on board this operation."

They started looking at each other, eyes impossible to read, but looked as if they were wondering if he was crazy or had something important to say. It took another drink, but Bowen laid out what he knew about their plans, his expression darkening, Browning in hand, his tone building with menace, pushing buttons, telling them, in short, their asses were grass.

They must have seen it coming, hands delving into their jackets, lurching to their feet, but Bowen took them out with one 9 mm hole in the head each, sending them tumbling back to the couch.

Easy.

He realized this stunt could come back to haunt him, but before the North Korean colonel got wind of the executions he should have enough time, coupled with the storm about to hit Chicago, to fabricate a plausible story.

He strode down the hall, contemplated keeping the woman around for another hour or so, then decided he'd rather have peace and quiet, the place to himself.

He needed to relax awhile, unwind, unencumbered by the mere presence of other folks, before he set out to lead the Iraqi charge.

5

Bolan's sweep of the complex ate up the better part of two hours. It was painstaking going from building to building, a top-to-bottom search, M-16 out and ready for the worst at each corner. But there were no more hardmen, roving or otherwise. Five dead gunners did turn up when he hit the command center, the soldier having a good idea who had waxed them, but only a seance would tell him the reason why. By then, Stony Man blacksuits had flown in, set the Kiowa down on the airfield. They assisted in securing all civilians in the main work building, calming them down, then went to deal with the state and local police.

The light show came whirling onto the funeral pyre about the time Bolan wrapped up his walk-through. Following the civilian roundup phase and head count of survivors, one of the Farm's blacksuits, thinking ahead, updated Brognola on the situation, specifically the human cargo whisked off to points unknown by gunships and the local law hassle about to come banging on the door. Springing into action on his end, the big Fed scrambled a team of FBI and Justice agents from Tulsa and Oklahoma City to secure the compound and its perimeter, and hold back overzealous or suspicious lawmen. Another eternity later it was all back under control, as far as Bolan could tell, but barely. And as far as the soldier was concerned, the mystery was deepening.

It was far from a clean wrap there and the soldier found himself impatient to get on with it as more questions swarmed in his mind. Bolan was aware, too, the ringmasters of this conspiracy were putting more distance between them and the scene of their crime with each minute. Where was the enemy going? What were their plans for the hostages? How, when and where would an army of Iraqi fanatics fit into the scheme? How big a terrorist army was about to be cut loose? Without question the Executioner needed to touch base with Brognola via the secured radio sat-link on the Kiowa, so the two of them could figure out how to proceed.

First Bolan decided to steal a few minutes asking his volunteers some questions, walk through the command center one last time. He was reentering the underground cavernous belly, choked with its camera banks and hanging monitors, when one of his volunteers, Carnes, said, "Agent Belasko. Looks like Turner left something for you."

"Turner?"

"Base chief, supposedly DOD's man in charge of the project. The cowboy who went bonkers outside and did his kamikaze number?"

"The cowboy?"

"Yeah. He always wore a cowboy hat. Look to you like John Wayne shot up his own gunslingers on the way out of here? But why?"

"Guilty conscience."

"He was one of them," Carnes stated.

"Way it reads. Radio system shut down, no way I can find to get any of it back up and running. You tell me all your cell phones are useless now, nothing but static?"

"He tapped in and jammed the works."

"Turner had the keys to the ranch. I figure he threw some switches somewhere, shut down any way to call for outside help. Only thing I see working are the radar monitors and the security cameras."

"All they wanted was to monitor the traffic, air and foot?"

"Right."

"While the men rounded us up or went and outright murdered the others in cold blood in the mess hall and killed the technician and labor force in their living quarters."

"It's stacking up that way."

The other volunteer, Harper, was working a disapproving eye over the camera monitors. "I can only imagine whatever kind of jollies Turner got down here. I always wondered why we never saw him around much. Look at this. These cameras cover every bathroom and bedroom in every home, every inch of space in every work area, more of them devoted to watching workers than the perimeter itself. Son of a bitch. Who would have ever thought? Big Brother lives."

"Lived," Bolan corrected.

"Right. Spying? Or peeping on the wives?"

"Probably both," Bolan said, and took the disk from Carnes. Bolan read "Belasko," then "Medusa" penned on the disk. Whatever Turner had been to the conspirators, it was clear something in the man had snapped. Apparently, or so Bolan hoped, the man had grown a conscience in the last minutes of his life, deciding to leave behind the mother lode of answers to this maze of a mess. Either way Bolan had some idea what had happened here and why. And if what he believed was true, then Bolan knew he was looking at a mass kidnapping of SDI elite, facing an international conspiracy that had roots somewhere back in Washington, and reached around the world to Baghdad.

Carnes looked at Bolan, the man still holding the confiscated subgun, nervous, as if some shooter he'd missed were ready to leap out of the shadows. "What in the world happened, Belasko? Clue us in, can you?"

Bolan heard one of his blacksuits raising him over the backup tac radio from the Kiowa. "Striker, our people just choppered in, touched down to handle the local problem, sir. Situation under control for the time being, but the ice sounds ready to crack from the way I read the talk."

"Tell the locals every inch of prairie for five square miles just became property of the Justice Department. If they want to keep their jobs, better yet, if they don't want to look at federal obstruction charges, they'll do what they're told and back off. Handle it."

"Roger, Striker."

"What's the total count on civilians?" Bolan heard the number, told the blacksuit he was on the way out and signed off. He repeated the number to his volunteers.

"That means they took thirty to forty of us with them," Carnes said. "But where? And why?"

"They were kidnapped."

"Kidnapped?" Harper said. "By whom?"

"North Koreans, working with a few folks from either DIA or NSA or both. Might even be a covert intelligence agency, something nobody's heard of, nothing you could find in the congressional book of records." Bolan wanted to add that it happened, but he could read their faces and knew they understood enough to believe anything was possible in spookdom.

"You're telling us," Carnes said, "that all this was maybe designed from the start of this project? Some inside job? To kidnap, what, the best of our ballistic missile people, our SDI brains? Working in collusion with North Korea?"

The Executioner had nothing but ideas based loosely on the few facts he had, but told them, "That's my thinking. Further North Korea's own nuclear missile program. ICBMs, killer satellites, the works. Get them on more than even footing with everyone at the top of the nuclear pecking order. I'm sure you remember Los Alamos, a few other stories about Chinese theft of classified nuclear intelligence. Chinese peddling influence around Washington. Buying schematics or more for the latest round of high-tech weapons of mass destruction."

Carnes nodded. "Saying anything is possible."

"Anything and everything. Let's get out of here," the Executioner told them. "I want you to tell me about yourselves, how you ended up here and exactly what was happening on this compound. *A* to *Z*, quick and concise. Don't leave anything out, even if you think it might be unimportant."

THOMAS SHAW COULD SEE a few of the abductees were near a breaking point. Somewhere in the packed crowd a woman quietly sobbed, a man rocking her in his arms. Close by someone was making strange sniffling noises, and somewhere else in the room, a man moaned, sounding more like a wounded animal than anything human. Two of the captives stared ahead, at nothing, crazed by terror, he believed, but looking paralyzed by their own sense of certain doom, floating away in despair. To Shaw they all looked dazed and confused, shell-shocked and consumed by nothing other than fear of the unknown. Who could blame them?

And, of course, their abductors had not left them alone. Two black-garbed thugs were standing watch somewhere near a small generator-powered light. The shroud of white fanned out, illuminated only the faces of captives, while rendering the armed guards as headless black statues.

Shaw was rapidly caving to the strain himself, insides knotted by his own fear—the horror and uncertainty—to where he wasn't sure what he was going to do next. But the latest shuttling of the group left him near despair for some reason. After the hollow ring of hope, there had been no armed cavalry on the way to set them free. He tried for the sake of his wife and daughter to keep the growing terror off his face, but it was hard to do that when they were all—thirty-six abductees by his count—left feeding on the silence, hearing the sobs and the moans, smelling the fear that seemed trapped by cracked concrete walls, while watched by faceless gunmen.

It was impossible to know exactly where they were,

but it was some type of underground bomb shelter. Built late forties, he reckoned, when the cold war was in full swing. The room smelled of ancient mildew, mold and dead things long since rotting away in the grimy subterranean cavern of whatever and wherever this black desert mountain was. He was thinking they were somewhere in New Mexico—perhaps a testing bunker or underground atomic shelter long since abandoned by official government or military, but one that their abductors had known about all along and had planned to hide all of them.

Until when? What next? How long before someone in the group cracked, made a suicide charge for one of the black-clad guards? What about food? Water? How were they supposed to relieve themselves?

Again, nothing to do but wait and worry, as he briefly rehashed this last leg of the journey. By his rough guesstimate they had spent between ninety minutes and two hours in the air. They landed at some remote airfield in a scrub-and-mesquite desert, ringed by black sawtooth hills. It might as well have been the dark side of a planet in another galaxy. Herded next into maybe ten vehicles, either oversize vans or black GMC trucks he'd seen used as official government vehicles for spooks. Another hour or so, bouncing over hard earth, then they were marched into a hole in the side of the mountain and down four long flights of steel steps. He recalled the rats he'd seen on the way down, as well as other furry creatures that crawled and slithered as they descended into a maze of concrete rooms. More barking for them to keep moving, more threats.

He searched out the faces, discovered Monroe and

Parker were no more than four feet away. How had he missed them sitting so close? He checked the armed shadows, unable to tell if they were paying any attention to him, but what did it matter anyway? The three of them, he believed, were the prize catch, and he felt guilty for a moment for feeling they were better than the others. He edged as quietly as possible on his haunches across the floor, risking it. "Blankenship was working with them," he said in a harsh whisper.

They were sullen, thinking about it, then Monroe nodded. Parker, darting a look toward the light, said, "The way he sounded and looked, I'd say so."

"He went AWOL from the base, sometimes two, three weeks at a stretch," Monroe added. "Always vague about where he'd been, never answered his e-mail or his cell phone when we needed to go over some work together."

"Can I trust you two?"

There. He asked the big question, point-blank, mustering all the penetrating steel he could put behind the words.

"With our lives," Parker said.

"We're not with them, Tom. You've got to believe us."

It was enough for Shaw, and he told them, "I do." He'd known these men since their early shuttle days at NASA, then later when they calibrated Tomahawk guidance systems used during the Gulf War. Of course, people could change over the years, with circumstances, desire and ambition charting new courses a man would never fathom himself capable of. But he considered himself a fair judge of men, and they had received no special consideration from their captors

that Shaw could see. A dark thought, alien to him up to
that point, tumbled through his mind. What if Blankenship was a traitor, going to the other side for money or
whatever bait he'd swallowed? What if he was involved
even on the periphery of what he and his family now
endured? Blankenship was dead, and perhaps that was
the only reward for his treachery he deserved. Shaw was
about to pursue another question, but it was as far as
the discussion went as a faceless voice boomed, "No
talking! Next person who speaks—"

The North Korean breezed through the doorway, as
if taking his cue, and finished the threat. "The next person who disobeys my order for silence and I will pick
two individuals—women I know for a fact are mothers—for punishment." He moved into the light, waiting out the silence, defying someone to challenge the
order. "On a more pleasant note, I regret you must lan-
guish in these primitive conditions. Such esteemed talent as yourselves deserve better. Soon you will be
leaving here. Soon you will be rationed food and water.
Again, you will go where you are told, do what you are
told. Heed this advice. You can accept your situation,
thus giving yourselves peace of mind, making it easy
for yourselves and comrades. Or you can fight it, make
it difficult. The choice is yours, and it should be an easy
one to decide. Life or death. No more simple than that.
Now, I am sure you are all wondering where exactly we
are going. All I can tell you at the present is to prepare
yourselves for a long and difficult journey overseas. As
of the moment I first addressed you, as a group you became the sole property and possession of the Democratic People's Republic of Korea."

A murmur of horror rippled through the crowd before the North Korean roared for silence. And Shaw felt the bile rising in his throat, light and shadow spinning in his eyes. He thought for a terrible moment the man was smiling his hideous mocking smile again. He couldn't be sure, nor did he care. His worst nightmare reality was just confirmed. They were worse than prisoners. All along they were meant to be abducted, transported overseas...

And held, a slave-labor force inside the Communist hellhole that was North Korea.

It was the most devastating blow yet. If they were successful in getting them safely inside North Korea, Thomas Shaw knew he and his wife and one daughter would never see America again. Shaw found he was shaking, and choking back a howl of pure rage.

"WE'RE OUT OF TIME on this one, Hal. What I'm reading here tells me Chicago is set to blow. Same setup as New York. Dawn. Rush hour. Iraqi time bombs marching into masses of innocent commuters, public buildings, setting themselves off."

"Jihad. These twisted bastards."

Having dialed up Brognola from the secured radio sat-link, Bolan was back in the Kiowa JetRanger's belly, his next move already mentally mapped out. A Chicago blitz was on the table. All he needed was to go over what he had with the big Fed, hope Brognola and the Farm could come up with the logistics, and he was back in the hunt. At least he had the next launch point.

But if he didn't beat the Iraqis in Chicago to the punch...

The Executioner had also gained some useful insight from Harper and Carnes, and briefly relayed what he'd learned to Brognola. They told him that DOD, working in collusion with some shadowy subdivision of DIA called the National Security Force, had sought out and contracted the country's elite rocket scientists. They also signed up aerospace engineers, shuttle designers from NASA, with a smattering of satellite technical assistants gleaned from NORAD and Nellis, with families and all brought to the Medusa compound in Oklahoma. All of it was hush-hush to the extreme.

There was high-tech gear and equipment that looked foreign to Bolan in the main work compound, and he couldn't even begin to tell Brognola what it was. But according to Harper and Carnes, the majority of the work was classified conceptualizing, computer mock-ups of Star Wars scenarios, putting together, in miniature scale, the nuts and bolts of killer satellites. The compound was also tapped into a cyberspace network where they *borrowed* other technology and classified data on SDI, all the latest brainstorms on tomorrow's weapons of mass destruction. In short, the complex was a gold mine of the country's nuclear-capability system, with a bona fide SDI program on the drawing board and very much a reality in the near future. Bolan recited locations of several classified bases to Brognola, who said he would march in the bulldogs to ask the hardball questions of base commanders, even make a few arrests if he could drum up charges that, if they didn't stick, would bring out the sweat, rattle a cage or two and force some career military brass or high-ranking spook to sing.

"Civilian rocket geniuses, our best and our brightest, handpicked by the snakes," Brognola said. "Control and manipulate the system, top to bottom. In our face."

"Engineered from the start. Thing is, we have a few names, but I'm betting it's only the short list. And the only sure way I'm going to get any answers about the North Korean-Iraqi angle is to thrash it out of the next bunch of savages."

Outside Bolan heard the babble of voices, but there was no edge of panic now that the threat of imminent death had been removed. Brognola's legal troops had moved in to begin cleaning up the mess, questioning survivors, getting names of missing personnel and retrieving whatever key documents or data might be stored on computers. It was somebody else's show from there on, Bolan knowing he had done all he could to save the night, exterminating a few rats, then handing the place, persons and things over to Brognola's people from Justice. If there was more to be learned, they would find it and get it back up the chain of command.

The Farm's pilots began working the controls now in the cockpit, and Bolan felt the bird lifting off to whisk them back to Tulsa, where Bolan's Gulfstream ride would take him to O'Hare. Unless he missed his guess, the Executioner knew Chicago was a few short hours away from erupting into a mass killing field. Then there was yet another alleged cell named by Turner in Los Angeles.

Bolan kept scrolling through Turner's revelations about a group calling itself the Phoenix Council, handed over five names from the NSA, DIA and

FEMA, their positions of hallowed authority, these men of unquestionable reputations—before now. Now they were traitors, the worst kind of cannibal to Bolan, and he wouldn't yield an inch of ground in battle or pull the first punch to hunt them down.

Brognola whistled at the recital, but his voice gained a grim notch. "Striker, these men are about as high up as you can get before you fall in line for the presidency. It makes me wonder who else."

"I'm thinking they're already gone, Hal."

"With the black helicopters in question."

"I smoked their play in Oklahoma. When I crashed the door to their powwow, I'm thinking the ones at the very top weren't planning on running off with the North Korean colonel. My hunch, they were going to be left behind to maneuver key political and military pieces of the puzzle in place Turner alluded to."

"I have the Farm already tapping into surveillance satellites to track down those birds."

"Never any doubt."

"Okay, figure even with an auxiliary tank, weight on board, and you say they were moving in a southwest vector."

"New Mexico. Call it 250 miles tops."

"Then what? If we're both thinking the cream of our missile technology and SDI crop is going to North Korea...you see my point."

"It's a long swim across the Pacific."

"Yeah, but before they even make it to the beach, those choppers have to land."

"If this conspiracy is as elaborate as it looks, Hal, they plan to pull off a vanishing act somehow, some way. My guess is the bulk of the hostages will be used as shields, if the bad guys are cornered when they land. But the Titan Four were the big catch from the starting gun."

"And the others are just what?"

"Armor," Bolan said. "There to help them get out of the country, but don't ask me how they plan to do it. I don't think Turner knew, or he would have said. Hard to tell, the guy was losing it at the end. He could have forgotten a few critical details."

"But we can believe his farewell speech?"

"I'll transcribe what's here over fax. Decide for yourself. It's erratic, his thoughts all over the place, but there's enough here to know I need to be in Chicago next."

"Tell me what you need."

And Bolan spelled it out. The long pause from Wonderland told Bolan he knew Brognola had a full plate, with time running out. Any snags, any guff from the authorities in the Windy City, Brognola stated he'd have the Man lay down a presidential directive on the right doorsteps. Carte blanche for Special Agent Mike Belasko.

"And then there's this suspected cell in L.A.," Brognola said.

"And there could be others."

"I'll put the alert out. I'm thinking San Fran down to San Diego, just in case this Turner left out one or two viper nests before his swan song. You know we'll turn up zip on this assassin, Robert Bowen, also called the Reaper."

"My man from New York is in Chicago—that's all

I know, Hal. Sheraton Chicago Hotel and Towers. Penthouse suite. Easy enough to check out."

"This Turner must have really flipped, knowing he'd carve up his buddies from the grave. Maybe he saw he was about to get cut out of the loop, you think? Maybe he had a bone to pick with this Bowen."

"Or some act of contrition, who knows. Whatever it was, I want this Reaper."

"Any suggestions how to handle it? Arranging a military flight, it'll take two to three hours for me to even get you on the ground in Chicago."

"Stakeout."

"Cover the hotel with a team, inside and out, top to bottom."

"A man working the lobby desk. Bowen starts moving, shadow him," Bolan said.

"Correct me if I'm wrong, but it sounds like this Reaper pushed a button."

"He's a cold-blooded killer of bad guys, his own, women and children. I've seen the type before. He's a key player in the game. If I can take him down breathing, I might get pointers to steer me in the next direction."

"Don't count on him throwing up the white flag."

"It's worth a try. This is bad news that's right now the only one clear and close in my sights. Get me to Chicago quick as you can, Hal."

The Executioner paused, didn't want to say it, but his old friend must have been telepathic as Brognola stated, "Or this country's worst nightmare has only just begun."

6

John "Doc" Wallace wasn't any fan of hurry-up-and-wait, not when lives—like his own—were on the scales and he couldn't be positive which way in hell they were tipping. A black operation had to launch when the clock struck twelve, or else.

No ifs, ands or buts.

He was tagged "the Doctor," or "Doc," by his DIA and NSA counterparts for good reason. Special security may be his field of expertise these days, but black ops was his claim to fame. And this black operation on the table was rife with assassination, the mother of all sabotage and a mixed bag of players waiting on him to get it together.

So it had to go down by the numbers, component parts in place to a man good to go at an eye wink, committed to victory or death. In other words, he thought, all movements choreographed to nanoseconds, the whole mesh in lockstep. Different parts, one body, but get and keep it rolling until the successful conclusion. One fly in the ointment, one overlooked glitch, and the operation went down in flames. He'd seen it happen, and he had the scars to prove it.

And three minutes off the clock, either way, could spell disaster. Three hours and change, like now, and it could mean a death sentence.

His own.

The whole hiatus on the tarmac, three hours and sixteen minutes past designated wheels-up, corkscrewed the paranoia deeper with each agonizing tick of the clock. It was quiet enough out there, as it should be, and he wondered why that alone bothered him so much. Area 19 was isolated northwest of Nellis, due west of the gunnery range for this one special-access program. Five square miles cordoned by electrified cyclone fence, the real estate was as heavily guarded as what the tabloids and civilians commonly referred to as Area 51.

But it felt too quiet in the desert beyond this dry lake bed, too dark even, with only a few halogen lights burning from the three massive hangars. It felt wrong, all of it, a stillness, a sort of seething immobility in the air leaving the National Security Force head of security wondering what hammer of doom was coming down.

Two pieces of good news to consider in his favor. Number one—the prototype GlobeSpecter had rolled out of Hangar One nineteen minutes ago. It was parked now on the apron, topped off with fuel, four Pratt & Whitney turbofans quietly humming. Between cigarettes and clock-watching, Wallace couldn't help but admire the one-of-a-kind bird. That was, of course, when he wasn't taking note of the twelve Delta Force men in black with M-16s posted near the gray nondescript block of the administration building.

Damn near a shame, he thought, to waste such a

marvel of supertech, as he ran an eye down the giant sleek black bird. GlobeSpecter was so classified that all he had known in the beginning of this two-year, seven-month, six-day detail was Northrop-Grumman and Boeing were the subcontractors. Knowledge, though, was power, and since his own men were assigned to stay glued to the hips of engineers, tech assistants, brainstormers and whoever else around the clock, they caught whispers in the wind. And since his security detail was armed with every manner of high-tech surveillance and countersurveillance gizmos, he often heard tidbits on the specs when the geniuses slaved away, on and off duty. Three-quarters of a football field, it was a hybrid between a VIP military jet and spy plane. More so, a bastardization actually, the way he understood it, between the SR-71, B-52 Stratofortress, AWACS and a Gulfstream C-20. A ten mile ceiling, for starters. Range was 11,500 miles, in-flight refueling receptacle. The fuselage skin was of radar-absorbent material, produced—or created—out of Area 51. Allegedly the classified alloy was amalgamated titanium, aluminum and a carbon composite he'd overheard called Jinzincon Olo 6. The superbird was supposedly invisible to radar, undetectable by even satellite surveillance, the jamming multimode equipment capable of sticking a finger into eyes in the sky, render them blind—or so he'd heard. A ghost ship, it could fly lights out, take off and land on autopilot. Stern to stem it contained a cargo bay, passenger cabin with fifty-five seats, war room, then flight deck. It would have made life a lot easier, he thought, if weapon systems of 20 mm

Vulcan cannon, those twenty-megaton gravity ther-monukes, were off the drawing board and situated, but Wallace knew a man couldn't always get what he wanted. Price tag on this puppy was twelve billion and change.

A pity its fate, indeed. Once—if and when—they were airborne, he could sound off a chuckle about GlobeSpecter's future. He'd picture the seismic shock wave that would topple all the king's men at the Pentagon when they learned of the bird's fate. Globe-Specter was doomed to claim a watery grave in the Pacific.

The second bit of good news, Wallace observed, his three ops were still by his side. Meaning they weren't blown. Meaning, so far, no Delta goons sweeping over them, relieving himself, Bide, Pender or Thompkins of their Beretta 92-Fs with sound suppressors, stowed in shoulder rigging beneath bomber jackets.

All systems looked good to launch, then the bad news. He'd been informed they were waiting on the latest arriving hotshot VIP to make his grand appearance before they climbed aboard and hit the air for Cheyenne Mountain. That could mean something or nothing. Not even Wallace or his security ops were ever privy to the identity of the VIPs they were assigned to guard when they were shuttled around the country.

Deepening his suspicion, he also had to wonder why his man—the big man—had stepped off the Globe-Specter after parking it, not so much a glance his way, then vanished into the admin building. Something smelled, or was there a legitimate rational explanation?

Whoever the VIP was, his black sedan had arrived, forty-four minutes ago from the south gate. Something about that mystery was tweaking the old nerves.

What the hell was taking so long? What could they possibly be in there hashing over? Wallace wasn't the nervous type. But he knew what was on the line, and if they were blown the Nevada desert was full of shallow graves of folks who didn't toe the line or shot off their mouths or betrayed a personal agenda where black projects were concerned. He knew, because he'd pulled the trigger himself, packed a few of those graves with persona non grata.

More bad news. Wallace had already received the double set of vibrations on his pager. There was a problem on the other end, and he never like hearing about problems. Calm down, he told himself. Major Temple was part of the team, he had everything to lose, namely his life, but everything to gain. Like a cool five million in cash, new identity, some island paradise of his choosing, no more ex-wife buzzards.

The good major deserved his slice of heaven, like the rest of them, of course, but Temple was in way deeper. The hero was bought and sold by the council before this thing was even gestated, the man first in line to drop into their net, in fact. And the major cherished his rep, a bonus for the council. With those skeletons in the closet he didn't want to see brought to light of day, Temple was the kind of guy who would rather eat his gun than see his image sullied. The mighty major—two wars under the belt, more sorties, medals than the RAF during WWII— had fallen, more of less, to the usual sins, sex, drugs and rock and roll. The major was nothing short of a god in Air Force lore, but if the man's idolaters only knew. Well, Wallace understood, playing God required money, lots of it, and Temple over the years had a lifestyle to maintain.

There they came, filing out, marching. No uniforms to declare branch or rank, just topcoats, briefcases, the usual. VIPs first, four in all out the door, the new guy, Wallace thought, reeking of Pentagon self-importance. White hair close to the scalp, ramrod stiff, he led the parade. Bigshot VIP gave the four blacksuited guards a look, and on the move by Wallace, said, "Lose the cigarettes before boarding. And no smoking in flight."

Wallace hit a deep drag, just to wash back the anger.

By the numbers now, forget the VIP, he'd show the guy smoke soon enough. The copilot climbed the ladder next behind the VIPs, then the control crew of three. The major was next, lugging the same aluminum briefcase as VIPs, all the classified docs, but with a little something extra in the package for the ride. Wallace had to admit he could see where the ladies would swoon over the guy, movie-star looks, lean and mean in his black pilot's jumpsuit. Wavy dark hair, Miami tan, he didn't look a day over thirty, though he was a few birthdays past the midcentury mark. Arrogant, too, standard for his kind, but Temple took the act to new Caesar vainglory.

Wallace let his boys take the ramp next, going with the program, VIPs peeling off for the war room. Up top, the major pulled up beyond the hatch, and Wallace heard "I need everyone assembled in the war room for a minute." A freeze, the sudden break in routine throwing off the flight crew as they balked in the hatch. Not good, but Wallace was climbing, mentally urging them to move it. They did.

"Problem, Major? We're already three hours behind schedule."

This was it. Temple trailing his crew into the white-green glow burning off the ringed banks of radar and surveillance and countersurveillance monitors. Once it happened, Wallace worried about one of those state-of-the-art eyes...

Nothing they could do about that kind of collateral damage.

Wallace hit the button beside the hatchway, the thin titanium ramp folding in sections, sliding under the fuselage, molding as part of the belly. A few more nervous heartbeats, waiting for the hatch to shut out the Delta goons, his pulse torqued up.

Show time.

Wallace squeezed through the hatch, into the war room, his guys claiming their posts. Bide and Pender on his nine, Thompkins on his three. Just in case, Pender was ordered to hold his fire, weapon by his side, monitor the major when it hit the fan. No flies. No glitches. No double Judas action, thank you.

Temple set the case on the teakwood top of the conference table, dialing the lock combination.

"If there was something to say, you should have done it during the briefing, Major. This bucks every shred of protocol and I want an explanation."

"A minor detail I needed to go over here, sir. Only take a few seconds," Temple stated.

"Let's have it, then."

The lid came up, Wallace taking in the sights one last time. Crew staggered to his eleven, VIPs dead ahead.

Picture perfect, then it went deadly sweet.

"There's been a change in plans."

Wallace had the Beretta out first, beating the major by a nanosecond, hitting the trigger again and again, spitting 9 mm subsonic rounds no sooner had the go phrase signaled the slaughter. His guys, as laid out, worked their field of fire, left to right, Crew taking head shots, point-blank, while Wallace kept drilling holes in VIPs the other way. The major came through, snakebite fast, but a flash of anger stabbed Wallace when Temple chose to drop the big shot first, one in the face. Shock factor had frozen them all, deer in headlights, and the last body was tumbling a few heartbeats after the gallows lever was yanked. A quick scan of the consoles, and Wallace breathed relief. Nothing sparked or smoked, only the bulkhead scarred with furrows from exit rounds out the brain, some greasy webs of crimson spreading over monitors.

The major scowled at Pender, slapping at some of the blood and muck that had shot over his jumpsuit. "Your weapon jam? No stomach, or is it something else I need to know about?"

Wallace ignored Temple, smiled at the big shot, whose face was a freeze frame of shock, blood dribbling off his chin. The guy had landed, dummy perfect and staring at nothing in one of the barrel wingbacks. "Who was that asshole, Major?"

"Some brigadier general. All you need to know is that he was important."

Wallace grunted. "Yeah, he looks real important now."

Temple dumped the Beretta into the case, snapped it shut. "Let's get this show on the road."

Wallace, Beretta holstered, clacked his Zippo, flame to the cigarette perched on his lip. He nodded for Pender to follow the major.

Temple scowled back at Wallace.

"Just so I can relax, Major," Wallace said. "Come on, we're all good buddies here. Same team."

THE REAPER HAD the place all to himself.

The Koreans were dead. Thumbs down for the whore, too.

All he had to do now was wait for Turner to ring his cell phone, tell him the half million was wired to Tokyo.

While he waited he partied. He hit the bottle of Seagram's straight and was flying now on the whore's blow.

It didn't get any better than this.

Too bad the party would have to end soon. The bottle was three-quarters empty, though the wet bar had plenty of backup. But there was business to take care of, hitting the streets, making sure the Iraqis did their jihad thing, and damn sure see he got his money even if he had to fly to Pyongyang and rip the colonel a new one, which he might do anyway, just for chuckles. Right then, he needed to pace himself. The night was young.

He was breezing back toward the living room when he froze, focused through the pounding in his ears and took a few seconds to figure out the sound. He was reaching for the unit fixed to his belt, but another trill, and it was coming from...

The couch! The colonel, he realized, ringing up the cell phone, only the North Korean Frick and Frack weren't in any shape to answer. Bowen felt his heart pulsing like a jackhammer from the core of his brain, face hot, sweaty. He weighed whether or not to answer when the noise died. How many rings?

He downed another drink, jumped again, this time the trilling in his ear. He plucked up his cell, thumbed it on.

Silence, then, "Why does Kim not answer his phone?"

Bowen chuckled. It wasn't quite who he expected, but maybe it was better than he could hope. Time to take the top brass by the throat. He'd never met the guy personally, but he'd seen enough intel photos and always figured the voice would match the inscrutable face of Bok Chongjin. Yesterday, when the future was dark and uncertain, he might have wondered how the colonel got the number only Turner had committed to memory. No genius when it came to math, he could still add two and two.

"Kim stepped out."

"And Jin?"

"Stepped out with Kim. I don't know where they went. Let me speak to Turner."

A pause, then, "Mr. Turner stepped out. I don't know where he went."

Bowen hit the bottle, chuckling. "Touché, Colonel."

"Then let us—how do you say?—cut the shit."

"That's how we say it."

"You are quite the rebel."

"One of the fallen, I'm on fire here, and I'm breaking out of hell. Let me spell it out—it's real simple. I want my money. Half million, Colonel, like Turner agreed to for this second round of your people's shit work. The account number is—"

Bowen felt his heart lurch when Chongjin recited it.

"When the job is done, Mr. Bowen."

"That was five hundred—"

"I know the amount. It shall be done."

"How come this is sounding too easy?"

"Lies, Mr. Bowen. After a while it becomes too difficult to keep all the lies straight. I suggest we speak truthfully to each other. Time is short, I am a very busy man."

"We've all got problems. So, what's this great truth?" he asked, bending and huffing up another cocaine line.

"Initiate from your end. Immediately. See the job through. Money in the bank."

"I'm supposed to earn my retirement nest egg, is that it?"

"Whatever you care to call it."

"How will I know you've kept up your end?"

"My operatives will see to it."

"Sounds like a bad plan."

"It's the only one you have."

"How come I can see Genghis Khan's army marching down the hall or waiting for me in the garage?"

"Finish the job there, and my operatives will take you to Los Angeles. No duplicity. A bonus fee following your visit to the City of Angels. My operatives will find you in the city. Go with them to Los Angeles. Do the job there first."

The line went dead. Bowen cursed. He took a minute, staring at nothing, weighing the moment, choices. Zero options. He wouldn't earn five hundred large holed up in the suite. So take his chances. He'd come this far, weathered worse, he figured. The colonel's operatives would find him, huh? No sweat. He'd handle them if they got hinky. What about his mystery guest? Oh, please, show up, Belasko.

He would thus keep the faith, all around, nothing else he could do. The job there was the key, then a bonus in L.A. Why not? Just keep his eyes peeled, gun hand ready, he was plenty alert as it stood.

Bowen shrugged on the midlength black leather coat, the kind he'd seen worn by shooters in the Russian Mob. It fit good, looked great, pockets deep enough for his purpose. From the war bag, he snapped up and filled a pocket with two fragmentation grenades, then fastened on a hip holster for the whopper, next nestled clips for the Browning and the Desert Eagle in his waistband. He checked the HK MP-5, cocked and locked, a pair of taped clips in place, ten doubled mags in the bag. He zipped up bag and coat, punched in the numbers for the shithole in the South Side where Wahbat Mazad was probably foaming at the mouth by now to get it going.

The familiar voice came on, guarded but gruff, "Yes?"

"Wahbat, how they hanging? It's your favorite ugly American. Saddle up, it's show time. Be there in a jiffy."

"Is it time?"

"What'd I just say? Yeah, it's time."

Bag in hand, the Reaper, fueled up and ready to kick any and all ass, flew for the doors.

He could always dance on more graves later.

It was time to go to work.

COLONEL CHONGJIN DIDN'T have time to spare dwelling on headaches he couldn't control. Chicago would have to take care of itself. Whether or not the DIA's treacherous killer made it to L.A. was of no consequence. This Reaper, he suspected, was greedy enough to chase his lust for the big payday, one he would never see, of course. Chongjin trusted his own operatives to close the assassin's account in due order.

Things were happening at lightning speed again, and Chongjin focused on the moment before more control of the entire situation—including himself—was lost. Their captives were being ushered out of the bunker, a stream of mass but silent hysteria marshaled back for the vehicles outside the hole cut into the mountainside. They had picked up an additional eight black-ops personnel from the secured New Mexico airfield, ten if he counted the two left to watch the remote compound. A paltry number of reinforcements, regrettably, to shore up a force already depleted. But they would have to take what they could get, he decided. They had only just begun to enter the real danger zone. From that point on, the plan would unfold, Chongjin knew, down from hour to hour, now minute to minute.

It was the five shadows of the council, holding their ground near the oversize van, that dug the new dagger of grim dread into his belly. They hadn't boarded, as ordered below, and as he closed he sensed a problem. He pulled up in front of the group.

"What is it?"

The retired FEMA man was clearing his throat, darting a look over the faces of the others, as if seeking encouragement to speak, then glanced at the captives being ordered by their operatives to get into the vehicles. "I'm electing to stay behind, Colonel. I feel it is in the group's best interest to stabilize the situation on this end, make sure we are all prepared for what's coming. I will remain on U.S. soil, shore up loose details, you understand."

"Keep things running smooth?"

"You're going to need one of us in the States to see the right strings keep getting pulled."

Chongjin nodded at the others. His hand was being forced. They knew it was impossible at this late stage, given the unforeseen disasters that had nearly toppled them out of the gate, for any one of them to stay behind. One wandering bailout might well demolish the entire operation, since there was a good possibility at that point the man left behind would get arrested, all manner of interrogation sure to follow by their various intelligence agencies. If one domino fell...

"Do you speak for the others?" Chongjin asked, raising his voice as engines revved, lights flaring on, a few pairs of eyes squinting as their faces were lit up. He read the uncertainty down the line.

They had argued briefly below on how to proceed. As far as he could tell, they had all readily agreed to fly with the ship that was destined to go down, then proceed to North Korea. It was too late to chart a new course, search out other solutions that might plug the hole in the cracking dam. They were all in this together or they were dead. How much simpler could it get? They knew this, or so he thought, men of ambition usually understanding crisis was simply a hurdle on the way to the greater reward. He had relented, though, on one point. There was nothing close to a sufficient runway there to land the plane. It was his original oversight, which was ordered in the heat of the moment when he sensed the present crisis on its way. They were moments away from making the jaunt back across the desert to the airfield, GlobeSpecter en route, with Chicago poised to blow as part of the plan to divert attention from the commandeered aircraft. There would be worry enough in the coming hours without having to deal with cold feet.

"You'll have to ask them, Colonel."

He didn't ask, but he searched their faces. Their silence was easy to read.

The retired FEMA man wanted out.

"So stay," Chongjin said, took his pistol out and triggered a round into the face of shock and outrage. Someone swore, the group lurching back as the dark spray hit one of them in the face. In the corner of his eye, he spotted his two operatives rolling toward him, reaching for weapons, ready to kill them all if that's what it took to keep the operation moving ahead.

Chongjin kept the pistol low but ready. "Choices, gentlemen, were made by you long ago. A commitment was made between us—I expect it to be honored. If you wanted easy you should have never agreed."

"So, there's one more parachute not to worry about," Jeffrey Hill said.

"I told him it was a bad idea," Henry Jacklin added. "We're too far along. You're in or you're out. Each of us knows too much about the others to run solo."

The matter was settled, all for none, he believed the Americans said—or none for all. "Then I believe we have a plane to catch."

The line was drawn, but Chongjin waited until they settled in the van before he claimed a seat.

7

Brognola's special Omega teams came through like champs, nearly landing Bolan on his enemy's back. The black Dodge Ram in question was presently crawling north up LaSalle Street, the wheelman IDed by Brognola's agents as the Executioner's man from Brooklyn. From the shotgun seat of the Crown Victoria, Bolan monitored the van, filling his combat vest with spare clips for his side arms, two flash-stun grenades going into pouches, while Special Agent Rankin maintained the slow crawl through rush hour quickly bulging up with traffic, four car lengths behind the target. Omega One was mirrored in the soldier's starboard glass, Bolan glimpsing the backup detail holding several car lengths to their six.

Were they all set for the tag and bag? Bolan wondered.

The Loop was where it would happen, an unnerving nagging in Bolan's gut swarming him with a sense of déjà vu that the lid could blow off Chicago, a repeat performance of New York, with terrorists running and gunning in the streets until they were nailed by police,

Feds—or the Executioner. Unless he missed his guess—and the Stony Man warrior hoped he was wrong, but instinct warned him otherwise—an undetermined number of Iraqi terrorists was about to take to the Chicago streets, open fire at random, maybe light themselves up with grenades or plastic explosives in densely packed mobs. Early-morning commuters, breakfast diners, trains and buses were all optimum targets, as were hotel and business lobbies bustling with teeming masses of unsuspecting potential victims.

Urban Armageddon was about to drop over Chicago unless Bolan and the Omega team got the jump and thrashed the snakes back into the bag. The Executioner needed a live one, either Bowen or an Iraqi, but he wasn't banking on the enemy to lie down with a whimper and give up numbers, names and locations. Either way, the soldier had come to Chicago with pretty much the annihilation of the terror cell on his mind. No punches pulled, he'd let the opposition decide whether or not they wanted to live to grunt their pain through a hardball Q and A.

The Executioner had mapped out the strategy and deployment, and Brognola had culled the four six-man Justice and FBI teams, the best of his best in Chicago, hauling them out of bed in the dead of night, placing them under Special Agent Belasko's sole command and authority. No questions, no exceptions. From top brass on down to the beat cop, Brognola had ordered the word spread that Bolan had carte blanche. No matter what happened. If anybody had a problem with that, they were to dial up the President, Joint Chiefs, or whoever they thought might listen to their gripes, but if they chose to buck the Justice Department's program they could start looking for another job at day's end. Chicago PD's twenty-five precincts were on full alert, with a joint Justice-FBI special task force claiming a command and control center out of the Daley Center. Security at major buildings of terrorism opportunity—such as Amoco, the John Hancock and Sears Tower, sundry museums and so on—was beefed up.

All roads, Bolan knew, led and ended at the Loop, the very piston that pumped the machinery of commerce, culture and politics for the Windy City. Brognola had agreed with the soldier during their meeting of the minds while he was in flight for O'Hare to fan the special teams in and around the Loop, roving armored vans, MP-5-toting agents and Feds with M-16s at their disposal parked on Michigan, Wacker, LaSalle and Dearborn. Then there were special Chicago plainclothes detail on foot, with SWAT teams hunkered down for bird's-eye surveillance—and possible sniping—at rooftop edges at the Federal and Richard J. Daley Center. They also had two police choppers in the air, ordered not to fly or hover below a thousand-foot ceiling, out of surface-to-air range for missiles, they hoped, unless the opposition had Stingers....

The Executioner wanted to believe it was enough show of force to give the Iraqi time bombs second thoughts about this being a good day to die, but his hunch was that the opposition was hell-bent on going the distance. Their jihad mentality wouldn't allow for anything less than the highest body count of infidels possible before they fulfilled their martyr's death wish.

Again Bolan had to walk through the mind of his enemy, as in New York. The Loop was analogous to the Big Apple's Midtown, in terms of commuters, endless targets of opportunity, the vitality and sheer importance of the area in question. All things considered the Loop was perfect for a murder spree. The Loop bulged with targets that, Bolan imagined, would make any terrorist howl in twisted glee. But to cover every building and street was an impossibility. CTA buses and subway trains would be jammed with the rush-hour throngs, with a number of platforms where some terrorist with nothing but mass murder in his heart could open fire and take out dozens of Chicagoans before they could even start to scramble clear. Then there were boats on the Chicago River that could take a rocket strike from the banks or from any number of bridges. Chicago was home to many world-famous museums, then there was the wide-open plaza of the Daley Center.

All of it opening now, business as usual, as the sun rose and the nation's third-largest city wakened to take care of the day's business. Or so they believed.

Bolan knew they were looking at having to cover around four thousand square miles.

A tall order, even in this high-tech wonder age.

Short of the President—backed by Congress—declaring martial law, rolling in the tanks, the Army and the National Guard, there was little the good guys could do except identify, hunt and take down.

The citizens of Chicago proceeded with their morning, and Bolan took in the crush of humanity, both foot and car traffic on LaSalle Street.

Bolan checked the positions of the other three teams

on the GPS monitor hooked beneath the dashboard. North, south and east, with Omega One completing the compass and all teams were marked, holding their turf.

Ready.

Bolan watched as Robert Bowen kept driving them around the city, as he had been for the past hour. Knowing the adversary as a pro seasoned in combat, Bolan could be sure they'd been made, Bowen feeling his nerves, maybe looking for a spot to unload his Iraqi death machine. They passed St. Peter's Church, grinding ahead in the traffic clogging up more the closer they crept to City Hall, due west of the Daley Center. The van went left, and Bolan hauled up the Uzi submachine gun from the war bag. He put his com-link with throat mike in place. He was snug, perhaps even a little weighted down in the black leather trench coat, but it was a special delivery attire requested from Bolan to Brognola. The coat was custom cut, slotted inside and out with extra pockets and pouches to hold still more magazines and fragmentation grenades. The coat was for both tactical purposes and appearance's sake when he hit the streets, in pursuit most likely and needed whatever critical few moments required to blend in with the citizens. The tac radio for link to Daley command center, a special frequency also on the digitalized minipanel for Chicago PD, was clipped on his belt.

That Phoenix Council, Bolan thought, had gotten this far didn't surprise him. Traitors, in his experience, were as smart as the devil, and covered their assets with cash and lead. Loose tongues were generally heard in short order, and ripped out of their mouths. Bogus passports had been next for the terror imports, cash spread around to the right people to grease the skids, then apparently the North Korean faction had aided in smuggling the Iraqis piecemeal into the States, the terrorists bringing along their women and children, settling in as part of the Arab community. Smoke screen, of course, but any bureaucracy was full of loopholes, and if an illegal immigrant was looking to dodge the routine naturalization process, it wouldn't take much effort to blend in as part of the scenery in the States and lie low. The problem was simple enough to identify on the surface at least. Bad guys almost always knew who the good guys were. On the constant lookout, they could duck and hide when necessary, outright lie when the need arose. And the terror imports were much like felons on the lam, Bolan thought. Unless a tip, anonymous or otherwise, was placed to the law, there was little the good guys could do except catch a lucky break, spotting the criminal in question on the loose or simply, unfortunately, wait for it to hit the fan, then rush onto the scene. All manner of constraints and restraints were heaped upon the law-enforcement officer by the Constitution, which, Bolan believed, was as it should be. The Founding Fathers were wise enough to know certain restrictions and responsibilities kept the darker side of human nature at bay, especially when it came down to wielding the power of the law.

Well, the Executioner wasn't bound by conventional tactics, Miranda and such. The longer he lived, though, the more he believed just how precious personal freedom was, but he'd also come to see the erosion of certain responsibilities inherent to bless that same freedom. There was, indeed, a very thin line in American society between law and order and anarchy. It was perhaps this thread the enemy had taken note of, now looking to slice it, with the violence they wished to unleash on American citizens meant to see armed revolution erupt, the people turning against a government they deemed incapable of protecting them.

Bolan couldn't read their minds, but their actions in New York had spoken loud enough for him to know that if American cities became war zones, with international terrorists blowing up buildings, machine-gunning civilians in the streets, then no one and nothing was safe, and the Constitution might be viewed by some radical faction as nothing more than paper with meaningless words. Fear would spread, coast to coast, panic swelling among the citizenry, cynicism toward the power structure spinning toward blatant defiance of the law and hatred. Once anarchy was unleashed, it could well avalanche into a nationwide revolt, Bolan feared, by an armed citizenry who saw the American way of life as they'd known it being snatched away by a foreign invasion of murderers and saboteurs.

The thin line.

Bolan's enemy either didn't know the city, driving aimlessly for another twenty minutes, or he had a firm destination—or ambush—in store. The van led them toward the river, finally swinging into an alleyway of an industrial park.

"Stop and wait," Bolan told Agent Rankin.

The Justice agent slid in by the curb. "And when the shooting starts?"

Bolan gave the man a look, measuring Rankin. If it weren't for the fact Rankin had a solid track record as an outstanding professional, the warrior might have thought the agent sounded miffed at being relegated the rearguard standby. Not so, the soldier judged. And there was no hidden message in the eyes, Rankin silently telling Bolan he didn't care much for any cowboy play. To an agent, they had been briefed thoroughly on the New York front, Bolan's role somewhat glossed over, but the sense Bolan had was that these agents under his command trusted him to make the right call.

"Then you'll be there to back me up."

"You got it," Rankin said.

And the Executioner was out the door, fisting the Uzi one-handed and holding it tucked inside his coat. Unlike New York, Bolan was right on top of his man this time, out of the gate.

The Executioner intended to finish it, one way or another.

HE WAS A KILLER, with more blood on his hands than Caligula and Herod put together, and he was damn proud of it. He also wasn't opposed to lighting fires, figurative or otherwise, when necessary. And Bowen had the sense he was about to become part of the city's bigger claims to infamy. History in the making, right, only his hallowed name wouldn't get penned in the books, even if he was an integral—no, scratch that, he decided. He was the Reaper, and he was the very badass thermodynamics behind this jihad.

Or at least that was how he felt before the buzz wore off. Heap on a craving for revenge, an overwhelming desire to vent rage and frustration, some electric itch up and down the spine demanding he kick ass, and Bowen couldn't ever recall feeling so bottled up and primed to go off. Human dynamite.

"Why are you taking us away from the heart of the city?"

"How many times you have to ask that, Wahbat?" Bowen snarled, hitting the brake, getting his bearings in the alley after checking the Iraqis in back. Clear to his twelve and six. Some industrial park, he observed, a sign reading Weeco Inc. hung from a fence near the lot that led to the river. What he found were at least two cross-running alleyways back out to either Randolph or Wacker or both. A definite plus, exits, since he knew they'd pick up a tail.

"Why are we stopping?"

Enough of this crap. Yulat had the shotgun seat, the Iraqi all but mummified with the wraparound bundles of C-4, wired to go, barking the question. Mazad and his companion from the apartment, Ahman, were in the back, throwing each other looks again, easy enough for Bowen to read bad thoughts where he was concerned. And Bowen felt his nerves jumping like exposed live wires now, sparks shooting up and down his arms.

He was in bad shape, all around, he knew, needing to get on with it somehow.

One, he didn't know Chicago nearly as well as he did New York, and it could prove a fatal lack of knowledge when he needed to bolt town, unless the next round of the colonel's flunkies found him first for that escort to their private airfield. He knew the Loop was where the Iraqis wanted to get dropped off. The Iraqis were edged out also, antsy to start the show. Time to kill, Bowen thought. Mazad, he recalled, had dawdled in the apartment, placing the calls to the other jihad troops, eating up time, making him wait, rubbing it in. Then Bowen was forced to malinger some more while the Iraqis took their sweet time getting wrapped and wired up, checking and double-checking AK-47s now stuffed in nylon bags.

Time was up for everybody. Before heading out of the hotel in the van, Bowen figured he had one more run left in him, and he was more than able and willing to blast his way out of the city, collect the biggest payday he'd ever see for bloodying up his hands for guys he wouldn't normally bother to spit on.

But now they had Feds nearly up their bumper, Yulat having pointed out the obvious a half-dozen times since they'd come up from the South Side. And Bowen hadn't missed the darting glances they'd shot each other during the whole jaunt over town. Okay, they didn't like his attitude, looking to put one in his head before they hit the streets, thanks a lot, ugly American, for the lift.

The morning, though, Bowen thought, was shaping up. It was a face back there in the Crown Vic he had filed away since Brooklyn. A face, he thought, that made his happy little heart flutter with anticipation.

Special Agent Belasko had come to town.

"That was the FBI back there!" Yulat nearly screeched, stare glued to the glass. "How?"

As if their ugly American was to blame.

Bowen saw Mazad reaching for the duffel bag, something changing in his eyes, downshifting from sinister to menacing. Yulat was just about to turn his way, head swiveling, when Bowen snapped out the Browning, jammed the muzzle in the man's ear and pulled the trigger. The 9 mm subsonic hollowpoint round tunneled through brain matter like some runaway freight train through drywall. The explosion of gore sprayed the interior, the other side of Yulat's skull going out a window that was no longer there, crimson glass slivers and blood washing the brick wall on the other side of his head.

Bowen was around and thrusting the Browning in Mazad's face before the blood drops could rain home on the shocked expression.

"Thou shalt not!" Bowen growled, then chuckled. "Thou shalt not fuck with the Reaper! Thou shalt not bite the hand that feeds! Thou shalt not blink or think treacherous thoughts! Now, go do your job! You and your boyfriend, get the fuck out of here! Go, assholes!"

Bowen saw them watching him, unblinking, but pulled the Browning back an inch or so as the Iraqis lifted the bags off the floor. "I'll see you in hell," he told them as the Iraqis hesitated, then Mazad threw open the door.

He waited a few moments, wondering if those two were stupid enough to set themselves off just to wax his butt, then something caught his eye in the side mirror, coming up hard and fast on his rear.

Belasko, he found, was double-timing it down the alley, swinging up the Uzi. Bowen's joy was brief, as the leadstorm came hammering up the starboard side, then started puking out glass, and screaming 9 mm hornets were tearing up the interior.

DISASTER HAD LANDED out of nowhere, and Colonel Chongjin took it all in through the reinforced, tinted cockpit portals as he yelled over his shoulder, "Get me the frequency of their squadron leader, Major!"

"I'm working on it, Colonel. Give it a goddamn second here. It's a classified military frequency they're on."

"Quickly!"

"Maybe you care to give it a try?"

He turned away from Temple's scowling face, left the man to his bank of monitors, the major working buttons and knobs, chasing through the static, skipping past local and state police bans, the jabber of official voices, of orders given and copied there, then gone.

It could have been worse, Chongjin briefly considered, but he couldn't see how. He wanted to feel grateful the behemoth GlobeSpecter had landed, waiting on the runway when they had returned from the bunker after the brutal, bone-jarring run across the desert. He wanted to thank his lucky stars all hostages were present, accounted for and safely under the watchful guns of their operatives in the passenger cabin. He wished he could feel blessed the parachutes were loaded in the cargo bay, another arsenal, complete with two hundred pounds of Semtex, under the roof.

For every positive, though, there was a negative. For every action a reaction. And Colonel Chongjin was right then staring down the sum total of his own imploding supernova about to suck him down at light speed into a black hole of no return.

There were more cop cars and flashing lights, more lawmen with shotguns and pistols, more military APCs and soldiers with M-16s, all of it strung out down the runway—in staggered formation to prevent even the most risky of takeoffs—than he could count. More Hueys and JetRanger gunships swarming the skies, more Thunderbolts, Tomcats and F-16s screaming in scissoring vectors back and forth.

Chongjin glanced down at the open nylon bag displaying its tools, the panel with the transponder and homing device lying between the pilot and copilot seats, a rainbow of wires severed now but coiling up as if to mock their plight. He nearly lashed out with a kick, but contained his anger. Self-control. Seize back the moment somehow. There was nothing they could have done about being tracked by Nellis and NORAD once they deviated from the flight plan. All of them had known once GlobeSpecter veered off course...

Still, Chongjin hadn't expected the Americans to act so swiftly. As preplanned, the transponder-tracking box was removed and rendered inoperable once the major had touched down to pick them up and had the time to disassemble the panel. Time was always of the essence, but Chongjin, reading the dark looks of the council aimed his way, knew getting stranded on the ground now would alter their own plans for the Pacific end of the ride.

"Mother Ship One, you are ordered to respond immediately."

The voice, authoritative and grim, jarred Chongjin out of pondering the darkness of the immediate future beyond New Mexico. He was looking at Temple as the major finished twisting a knob, punching a button. Temple stood, moved away from the console, gesturing that it was Chongjin's show.

"This is Captain Barker, Ranger White One-Five-Seven. You are to respond immediately, Mother Ship One, and you are hereby ordered by the United States

Air Force High Command out of Nellis to vacate the vessel."

Temple tapped another button, nodding at a small box on the instrument panel. Chongjin stepped forward, said, "Listen to me very carefully."

"Who am I speaking with?"

Chongjin paused, the cockpit shuddering as a pair of F-16s screamed overhead. "I am the man who has enough explosives to turn your GlobeSpecter to burning scrap."

Radio silence.

"I assume you are listening now, Captain?"

"Go on."

Chongjin felt the smile wanting to come on, but the moment was up for grabs. "Whoever your superior officers, I strongly urge you to contact them immediately. Should anyone attempt to forcibly enter, should they even approach this aircraft, I will order it blown up. These are my demands, and should they not be obeyed, I have almost forty of your best and brightest SDI talent on board. They are hostages, and there will be no negotiating their return. Should you not clear the runway within thirty minutes, I will begin a demonstration, should you need further convincing. For every minute you block our takeoff, I will choose one hostage and shoot them. I will start with the women."

"My orders are clear. You are not to leave this runway. You are to deplane immediately and surrender."

"Or else what? You blow us off the runway? You would kill American citizens your Department of Defense has invested millions of dollars in? You would risk losing a prototype, twelve-billion-dollar aircraft? I urge reason at this time, Captain. I urge you to contact your superiors and clear us for takeoff. I would also suggest," Chongjin said, aware he was putting himself at risk to have his next bluff called, "that you turn all your energy and focus toward a developing situation in Chicago. Should you force my hand, I am prepared to cut loose certain forces in other cities. I will open the gates of hell of urban warfare on your country with just one radio call, and I hasten to add this legion of mine is armed with weapons of mass destruction. As in anthrax and nerve gas. You are in what I believe you would call a lose-lose situation."

The response was long in coming, Chongjin scrutinizing the nervous glances the four remaining heads of the council threw each other.

"I'll get back to you, Mother Ship One."

Chongjin smiled at his American counterparts, thrusting out his arm, checking his watch. "You now have twenty-eight minutes to comply, Captain. Or I will blow your aircraft clear into the next state."

Another long pause, then, "I'll be in touch."

"Twenty-seven minutes."

8

The Executioner put the Uzi to gruesome work as soon as the two jihad soldiers hit the alley. To some small extent, Bolan would admit this was slightly personal. He had seen enough of Bowen's indiscriminate butchery in Brooklyn, women and children every bit fair game as their terrorist husbands and fathers, and the soldier wanted to be the man who bagged the traitor who did these dirty deeds for the Phoenix Council. And he'd lost Bowen once already, galled by the fact the man was still alive, murder his only game, no telling how many lives he'd snuffed between New York and Chicago or how deeply involved he was in laying the foundation for wholesale slaughter.

Never one looking to hero the action or ever seek the first shred of accolades, either, the largest part of the soldier remained professional, cold and committed to the task at hand.

This was duty, no more, no less.

And that called for putting the enemy down for good. Omega teams were spread around the Loop, and it was their play once—if—more terror dragons sprung out of their holes, breathing the fires of slaughter and mayhem.

Something appeared to bulk up the terrorists, Bolan saw. Their leather jackets were too tight a fit for slender builds, movements stiff, robotic. The Executioner heeded the warning bells of his combat senses.

They were walking human bombs.

Head shots, then, not a problem.

Bolan nailed one of them off the starting line, concentrating the short 9 mm barrage on the wanna-be martyr's head, exploding skull and brains, driving the near headless jihad gunner into the back side of the second man. By then, the other one had lurched into a sprint, the corner of a bisecting alley lending him immediate sanctuary.

Gone for the moment, but the Executioner had bigger game behind the wheel of the van.

A mental picture of Bowen at the helm, and the Executioner poured on the subgun fire, hell-bent on turning the van into a hearse. First, a burst through the open starboard side door, then Bolan shuffled across the rear, blasting in windows, going for broke with a long fusillade, swarming the van with ravenous steel-jacketed rounds, aiming for the driver's side. For a moment, spraying the port window with a vandalizing burst, he wondered if he'd scored. Then it was instant replay of the Brooklyn scenario, and Bolan wondered if these guys didn't all go to the same *Road Warrior* school of race and squash, points for pedestrian hit-and-run kills.

The engine revved, the vehicle shooting back in Reverse, there was a flash of demon eyes in the fractured side glass and Bolan was running, firing the SMG on the fly.

No tag of Bowen yet, as the van shaved off the thirty

or so feet in a rapid revolution of squealing rubber, a runaway bulldozer now, tail end zigging and zagging as the hardman got him lined up for roadkill.

Bolan spotted the Dumpster, charging, then hurled himself off the ground, the bumper locked on to his path, black steel blurring at him in the corner of his eye, growing into some juggernaut of doom. He was falling, headfirst for cover, when the metallic minefield blew in his face. The soldier felt his head smack some edge that was thrust his way from the impact, plunging his senses down into a maelstrom of shattered light. Bolan nearly winked out, but adrenaline came back, high voltage in the blood, pumping him through the pain and clawing darkness, snapping him out of it.

It was going to hell in a hurry, Bolan groping through the plastic bags for his Uzi, com-link askew on his head. The SMG was wedged between sheet metal and bulging plastic, and he was pulling it free, rising, trying to get his footing when the van plowed into the Crown Vic. It was a broadside smash, a nanosecond of sound and fury. Glass shattering, the Crown Vic was lifted off its wheels before slamming into a delivery van bogged in traffic. Bowen had been braced for the collision, but the warrior couldn't find the bastard behind the wheel. Any concern for Rankin in the Crown Vic was short-lived, but hot anger flashed through the soldier at another display of brutal indifference to life by Bowen.

Bolan kept slipping back into the bin. He thought he saw something chucked out the window, and Bowen was popping up now, screams and horns a meshing din. The Executioner lost a critical heartbeat to retaliate, feeding the Uzi a fresh magazine next, cocking and locking, sliding back down as his feet crunched through garbage giving way to his weight.

A double-billed rolling wave of thunder, but merging as one noise, left Bolan unable to discern if it was the van roaring back his way or some other racket he should have recognized. No time to pin it down and wonder about the next round of wailing and anarchy that was out of sight. Bowen was racing back to wax him and leave him buried for the day's trash pickup.

Bolan nearly had the Uzi up, target almost locked on, when Bowen cut loose with an MP-5, sweeping the SMG back and forth, the gunner's chin hugging the dashboard, subgun above the fist gripping the steering wheel. Bullets spanged metal, slicing the air above Bolan's head as the van carried Bowen's full-auto charge on top of the Dumpster. Bags erupted in the warrior's face, the hot lead driving Bolan deeper into the garbage for cover.

"Omega One to Omega Commander! Come in!"

Rolling out of the bin, Bolan adjusted his com-link, snarling a curse as the van whiplashed around the alley corner. He stayed his trigger finger on the Uzi, keyed the com-link on the run toward the crumpled shell. "Belasko here! Our man's headed north, I've got another hostile on the run, same direction!"

"I've got casualties, Omega Commander! Two civilians, three of our own men down! Goddamn it! That bastard blew us out of our boots, flung a grenade as soon as we fell out!"

Bolan picked up the pace, one eye on the Crown Vic, the other taking in the chaos to his three o'clock. At least two civilians were stretched out by the curb, crying out their pain, limbs bloodied, faces streaked with crimson. The damage done was even worse as Bolan panned the scene. The Omega One van had been dumped on its side by the blast, wedged now between two battered vehicles. Flames licked at the punched-out hole of the engine housing, fire eating toward fuel dripping from a ruptured line. Pandemonium swirled around Bolan. Gawking horror. Shouts and screams sounded, motorists laying on horns out of panic, terror or confusion. Omega agents, the Executioner spotted, were dragging their wounded onto the sidewalk, Agent Connors was bellowing at motorists in the vicinity to get out of their vehicles and run like hell. They did. Balaclava helmets had been knocked off two Omega agents, while their teammates—one of them bloodied about the face and limping—were feeling around the neck for a pulse, but Bolan knew they'd just lost at least two good men.

The van blew apart, dispersing fire, smoke and debris in all directions in what struck Bolan as some anticlimactic mockery. A red mist dropped over the Executioner's sight after he ducked beneath the front of an abandoned SUV, wreckage winging overhead. Citizens kept wailing, decibels rising to pitched panic.

The Executioner felt his blood freeze.

The war had started.

He focused on the groan from the Crown Vic.

"Rankin?"

The agent was sprawled across the front seats, grimacing at Bolan. "My leg...I think it's broken...."

"Help's on the way."

"Get me up!"

"Sit tight. You're out of it."

And Bolan made out Connors calling for an emergency medical team.

Unless they got damn lucky, the soldier feared Chicago would see itself maxed out on EMTs before it was over, hospitals stuffed with walking wounded, morgues packed wall-to-wall with bodies.

Bolan was jolted by a wave of shrieks and the blistering chatter of autofire up the block. With his Uzi coming around, the Executioner pinned down the new round of chaos, the scurrying of Chicagoans up and down sidewalks, dashing through lobby doors, hunkering down wherever they could find instant haven from slaughter.

It was the jihad soldier he'd missed. Bolan saw the killer firing an AK-47 into vehicles, then swinging the assault rifle around, shooting on and bellowing in Arabic as he bowled down citizens in a clustered herd.

The Executioner began threading his charge through the logjam of vehicles, the scurried maze of civilians. Okay, he decided, the enemy had a death wish. No problem. They wanted war, they wanted death, so be it.

Wherever the butchers stood their ground, Bolan would see their martyr's dream come true, something to ponder on their way to hell.

IHMAN JABAT BELIEVED he would laugh out loud, a voice like rolling thunder, the spirit fueled with righteous rage. He was the sword for delivering the truth and justice of God to his enemies. Before now, he had seen himself as some avenging Islamic angel of death in his mind's eye, floating through the air, defying gravity and all things mortal, this supernatural holy entity of judgment day descending from the heavens to slay earthbound demons.

A hero, a true son of the Prophet.

The reality was a far cry from his fantasies.

Now that jihad was mere moments away, his hands about to be stained with the blood of his hated enemies, he felt more fear—mingled with some malevolent uncertainty—than anything else. How could this be? he wondered. Wasn't he a holy warrior, the instrument of God's will to carve the cancerous, corrupting spawn of the devil from the earth? The sudden feeling of terror made no sense. Fear of the moment? The act itself, resulting in a body count that would prove a sorry disappointment to the river of blood he desired, thus his whole life, centered on this single defining moment, stamped throughout eternity as a putrid waste? Or was it fear of what waited beyond in the great unknown? Though he was positive he would soon bask in the blinding brilliant glory of God in paradise...

Or would he?

It shouldn't have felt like this, he thought. For more than a year—enduring the masquerade as a dishwasher at an Italian restaurant near where he lived in the ethnic mosaic they called New City—he had looked forward to this call to holy war. Indeed, the craving had swelled by the day, until he had recently contemplated simply walking into where he worked and cutting loose with an assault rifle. But he had stayed the course, remaining true to himself and the others, suffering in silence, smiling through the indignity and shame of his life in this country. Bobbing his head and kissing ass where required, no less, like some obsequious, ignorant peasant for all those native-born Americans he needed to suck up to and fawn over in order to keep them from becoming suspicious of who he really was, the true nature of his immigration.

The hatred had always been there, of course, even before what the devils called the Gulf War. How many fellow Iraqis had he seen murdered during the withdrawal from Kuwait, that sandspit, bulging with black gold nonetheless, that rightfully belonged to his country? How many family members killed or maimed when the hostile crows came squawking over Baghdad to bomb the city back into pre-Babylonian Sumer? Too many.

He had to try to balance the scales of justice.

Then there were the dreams lately, he thought, of slaying Americans, so alive in his mind at night, playing out in the sleep of yearning and revenge, seething visions of carnage and mayhem, with Ihman Jabat the warrior-god dispensing justice to the enemies of all Iraqis. There were mornings even, he shuddered to recall, when he'd wakened aroused, left wondering about himself in a fleeting moment of shame, then praying to God to grace him with some degree of self-control, even though it wasn't his fault. God chose not to answer that particular prayer, and the dreams of slaughter and subsequent erections persisted until he feared he was going insane.

Yes, he would die soon enough, he knew, casting as many infidels into the fires of hell as possible before he soared to paradise in martyr's glory. Yet the smallest whispering of a voice in his head seemed to demand he question what he was about to do. Shake it off, he told himself, nothing else to do now, topping the steps. Too late now, there were no alternatives, destiny already mapped out, having tugged and pulled him to this time and place. Fear, he thought, was understandable, even forgivable, considering the sacrifice he was ready to make in the name of God and all of holy Islam.

It was time to give back.

Jabat stepped onto the platform at Adams station, then slowly weaved his way through the mob of commuters waiting for the El train, proceeding for the northernmost edge. A look back, and he found Abudah al-Tehmada, appearing grim and burdened by the weight of his own large nylon bag, shuffling for the opposite end of the platform, as agreed. They would catch them in a scissoring cross fire, aware many of them would run for the stairs when the shooting started. There would be no escape, not for them, not for two holy warriors acting out the will of God.

Head bowed, Jabat muttered, "Excuse me, please, excuse me, thank you," edging toward his post. A quick look at the packed mass, down the platform and thronged near the tracks, and he believed God could not have blessed him with any better fortune. A year had proved an eternity to wait, fearing all along the moment when the FBI would come storming into his apartment or crashing into the restaurant, some neighbor perhaps calling the police, profiling him as a terrorist, simply because they didn't like the way he looked. But that, he believed, was simply America.

Well, the eternal wait was over. The call to arms

from Mazad came in, and the van with four fellow holy warriors was on its way to the Daley Center.

Perhaps it was a good day to die in the name of God.

He settled the duffel bag on the platform, scanning the crowd. They appeared dead to him, not even the in-human beings or the wild-eyed, soulless animals he wanted to find. All of them were either antsy or frozen in place, to an individual devil lost in their own thoughts, the concerns of the day ahead. They were young and old and middle-aged, men and women, well-dressed in fancy suits or shabby and scuffed in the jeans and work boots of their blue-collar workforce. White, black, yellow and in between, it was their ethnic melt-ing pot, a hodgepodge of peoples and clashing her-itage, he decided, alien to the point of abomination in his own culture. Iraqis would always be one people, under one god.

But he had detested Chicago from the very first day he arrived. It was intimidating, mean and aggressive in all its racing, seething energy, capable of swallowing weaker human beings with its vast sprawl and driving greed for more, to get or to take what someone else had. He had al-ways felt alone, somehow despised, not even another number in the crowd worthy of a remotely decent life. Viewed in contempt. No more. He was about to change all that, and forever, perhaps his very name immortalized when the glory of what he'd done in America reached Iraq.

Speaking of the glory of this moment at hand, he re-called the final words of the North Korean colonel be-fore he had shipped them off to Lebanon or Syria for last-minute shoring up of logistics.

"When you arrive in the land of the barbarian, you

will be justifiably appalled by many things your eyes will not be able to believe, much less stomach. They'll be every bit as demonic as you had imagined. Lust, greed, disrespect, racism, a land where even their own children murder one another. You'll see, to begin your journey while waiting for jihad, all that they have in terms of wealth and privilege, a mockery of your own lives, your former greatness, which, you must remember at all times, was taken from you by them. You'll see their great and imposing cities, forever rising higher to the sky, their animal desires always expanding and consuming, even now reaching across the oceans to subjugate other peoples and contaminate their cultures, threatening to reduce civilized Asian and Arab countries to poisonous cauldrons of wretched excess and immorality.

"The barbarians, they desire little more than instant gratification, living only to fulfill their need to rape the world to sate their wants and hold on to all their obscene wealth. You'll see a seething legion that wishes only to have more wealth, more power, more control, and at the expense, the blood of my own nation, and yours. You'll wonder how each one of them seems to have become their own god, erecting individual worlds of money and power and prestige, so that they can isolate themselves from family, while they turn a blind eye to the rest of the world's suffering. I tell you, they have exchanged—no, they have forsaken—character and moral principle at the altar of their swollen egos, out of all rational proportion to what they are really worth in terms of humanity. You must remember who you are and what your mission is. From what I know of your history, you

PLAY THE
Lucky Key Game

and you can get

FREE BOOKS
and a FREE GIFT!

Do You Have the LUCKY KEY?

Scratch the gold areas with a coin. Then check below to see the books and gift you can get!

YES!
I have scratched off the gold areas. Please send me the 2 FREE BOOKS and GIFT for which I qualify. I understand I am under no obligation to purchase any books, as explained on the back of this card.

366 ADL DNWA   166 ADL DNV9

FIRST NAME	LAST NAME

ADDRESS

APT.#	CITY

STATE/PROV.	ZIP/POSTAL CODE

 2 free books plus a free gift   1 free book

2 free books   Try Again!

BUSINESS REPLY MAIL

FIRST-CLASS MAIL   PERMIT NO. 717-003   BUFFALO, NY

POSTAGE WILL BE PAID BY ADDRESSEE

GOLD EAGLE READER SERVICE
3010 WALDEN AVE
PO BOX 1867
BUFFALO NY 14240-9952

NO POSTAGE
NECESSARY
IF MAILED
IN THE
UNITED STATES

have done more for mankind than anything the Great Satan has ever accomplished. Your land is the birthplace of civilization. Your ancestors of Mesopotamia created the wheel, gave the entire world the written word, the sixty-minute hour. You were the first of farmers, herdsmen and the finest of craftsmen. And they were warrior-kings, gods among mere mortals.

"And now what do you see in your once mighty land? A nation of proud people smashed to near ruin by your enemies. Disease and starvation, families you cannot feed, wasting away before your eyes. Devastation of a great city, no jobs, a begging legion of wretched homeless. They, the Great Satan, will not even allow you to barter oil for food and medicine. It is, I tell you, part of their devil's work for genocide of the Iraqi people. But you can, and will, strike back. You will soon soar above the crushed and broken bones of their bodies. Remember who you are, and from where you came.

"Go forth now, and perform the duty that has been laid out before you. You may call it holy war, that is your choice, but what you are about to embark on will help to create a better future, one that is good for the whole of mankind, one that will assure glory and honor to Islam, as well as my own country. The future—you perhaps will not live to see it—is there for the making for the next generation of your own blood, all of whom are looking to you to bless them with renewed life, to give them hope through your strength. You are warriors. You will go forth as lions among the jackals. You are the very embodiment of hope that arises from the ashes of your country's ruin. Go forth and be glorified."

Jabat snapped out of his reverie as he heard the train thundering down the tracks. He was about to bend at the knees, somewhat afraid to move his torso, wondering if sudden movement might set off the packets of plastic explosive wound around his chest, when he spotted the policeman. Something angry and determined in the policeman's eyes, the mouth moving around the radio held to his face. And Jabat found yet another uniformed cop shoving his way through the crowd, approaching Tehmada's blind side. How did they know? Or were they even after the two of them?

The cop coming closer now, eyes dropping toward the bag, his hand reaching for the holstered weapon. Jabat stooped, practically ripping the zipper off the bag, wrenching the AK-47 free. He shoved two, maybe three commuters away, gaining clearance to stand his ground and fire freely. Where was the policeman? The cop was gone—then Jabat saw him reappear as he pushed through the crowd.

Jabat heard a woman scream, "He has a gun!"

The cop, frantic, shouted, "Freeze!"

But he was already holding back on the trigger of the assault rifle, sweeping the muzzle around, tearing apart bodies, knocking them down in writhing heaps to the platform. He wasn't sure, but he believed he heard the stutter of Tehmada's Kalashnikov from the other end, through the roar of panicked shouts and screams.

No matter, this was the beginning of the end, alone or together.

A stampede for the stairs began, bodies toppling as he raked the mob with autofire, the train pulling in, gaping horror pressed to the windows and doors. Somehow, Jabat glimpsed the policeman falling for the platform, uniform shot up, blood flying. It was something of an accident, perhaps blind panic guiding his AK-47 to drop the policeman, freeing him to continue the massacre. Jabat took it in stride, not missing a beat, the death of armed opposition a blessing. Whatever he could get now, it was all simply a sign from above he was on his way for immortal glory in paradise.

SECOND-GUESSING WAS a luxury, Bolan believed, best reserved for spectators or the losing side. They—FBI brass, press, politicians, the TV commentators and maybe even the attorney general hammering down on Brognola—would Monday-morning quarterback this one to death. The "should have and could have" crowd would make a strong argument, just the same, about the horror show, the failure on the part of those in charge, loss of life somehow the fault of the good guys. So they would parade themselves through the talking-head spotlight, backbiting, second-guessing, pointing fingers, covering ass. Should have dropped the net over Bowen at the hotel suite. Should have issued a city-wide alert and insisted all citizens remain at home. Seal up the city, lock down all businesses. Should have had the National Guard, the Army, the Marines, Delta, SEALs inside the Loop and all the way out to the suburbs...

And so on.

Never one to pass the buck, Bolan could take the heat. It was his show, thumbs-up from Brognola, who had passed on the tough call from the Man in the Oval Office. With or without him, Bolan knew it would have gone down more or less the way it was erupting. The terror imports had been inside the country for some time, stashed, armed and marched out by traitorous jackals inside the very government and intelligence infrastructure that would sound off about the whole mess when the smoke of battle finally cleared.

Talk, Bolan knew, was always cheapest when the other guy could watch it all from the sidelines.

The jihad soldier was now hauling ass across Wacker, triggering off wild bursts, spinning this way and that, hosing down vehicles and pedestrians, creating a glass-and-blood shower. Bolan had cut the gap while the gunner took some time to act out his psycho fantasies in the middle of the street. The noise of the rampaging chaos was deafening Bolan, but the soldier's death sights were aimed on the enemy.

Civilians stampeded pell mell, rocketing across sidewalks, dropping for cover in vehicles as the jihad hardman shot out windows, kept spraying crowds and clipped a few more pedestrians off their feet on the run. All sound was a fractured roar in Bolan's ears, his tac radio squawking, the bleat of rotor wash from some distant point beyond the towering monoliths, sirens wailing from all points.

Weaving his charge between stalled vehicles, the Executioner was lifting the Uzi when the jihad shooter, as if sensing his nemesis closing hard, whirled and triggered a long burst across Wacker. There were too many innocent bystanders clogging any clean field of fire, bodies whipping all over the place, so Bolan dodged the line of tracking bullets. He went down just as steel-jacketed slugs pounded the frame of a Towncar, raining glass over the cowering occupant hunched beneath the wheel.

Up and moving out, Bolan wanted to believe there was nowhere for the jihad soldier to run.

Then Bolan found the man bolting onto the Orleans Street Bridge, and the target of opportunity loomed on the other side.

The Executioner gathered speed as the enemy ran on, hunching low between the vehicle logjam, feeding the AK-47, Bolan suspected, with a fresh pair of taped magazines. Off to roughly his two o'clock, Bolan took in the massive granite face of the narrow-windowed Merchandise Mart. And the jihad gunner, Bolan knew, was primed with God only knew how much high explosive.

Again the civilian traffic on the northbound one-way river crossover was blocked off as any easy tag of the enemy. The Executioner, crouching between vehicles as the enemy came up, firing, roared at trapped motorists, "Get down!"

The man started laughing, a psychotic hyena, spraying an extended burst, blowing in windshields. The flying glass drove Bolan to deeper cover as the lethal wave rolled on.

9

Adnan al-Bahkar had once heard the staggering numbers on the loot they had hauled out of Kuwait, booty, in his mind, that had always rightfully belonged to Iraq, since the Kuwaitis had simply been squatting on land that never really belonged to them in the first place. Sixty-five tons of gold coins, a little over 3600 bars of gold liberated from filthy-rich Kuwaiti hands to start. Then there were the ten-thousand-plus luxury vehicles, not to mention priceless paintings, other artwork and furniture—a few divans alone worth the combined lifetimes' pay of the entire Republican Guard—given to Kuwaitis by British royalty. In short, anything of even the smallest value that wasn't nailed down went back to Baghdad.

It was the vehicles, though, that always got to him the worst. Bahkar knew all about the luxury wheels personally, having steered a Rolls-Royce all the way back to Baghdad right before the American jackals had landed and started shooting up Iraqis who were only reclaiming their own property. Instead of medals for his valor and heroic service to Iraq, he had hoped their leader would have seen fit to bestow him with the gift of the Rolls-Royce, since he had gone through all the trouble of shooting the owner and his family himself, then risking his own life getting blown off the highway by some American fighter pilot en route.

It never happened. Like the other ten thousand rich sheikhs's handsome wheels, their president auctioned them off to cronies and other supportive allies from various Arab countries, raking in a whopping—so he heard—150 million dollars.

One stinking lousy Rolls-Royce—that was all he'd wanted. It was a far wail from the Chevy van he now manned, and he briefly found this sudden pang of nostalgic regret bitter strange. Was this the phenomenon peculiar to those American soldiers of the Vietnam War? A flashback? Well, whatever it was, he had been denied his due before, but destiny—God's will—worked in mysterious ways indeed. For instance, there were plenty of expensive cars jamming up Dearborn Avenue now. That red Jaguar, for instance or that black Cadillac. There was a Mercedes—gleaming spit-and-polish silver—driving his anger deeper, bringing on the Rolls-Royce flashback.

Something snapped inside as he glanced at his three brothers-in-jihad, Sakbah cradling the AK-47 from the shotgun set, the other two looking glued together in the back, their own assault rifles resting near the top of open duffel bags. Something—most likely the jihad had begun—had snarled traffic, infidels out and rubbernecking down Washington Avenue. And with the plaza so close, swarming now with their hated hordes bustling for the Daley Center, the very heart of the Cook County judicial system.

It was time. If, he decided, he could never sit behind the wheel of a rich man's car, he could at least ruin somebody's else day. Three months of hard labor in a warehouse near the river, snapped up by the North Koreans from the beginning, and the van was finally rigged and wired to blow with 220 pounds of C-4. He would aim for the lobby doors, of course, but the boom he was prepared to drop would sear across the plaza and hopefully vaporize some rich pig's cherished ride.

"Go!" he roared, taking the radio detonator box out of his coat pocket, thumbing on the red light.

They were out the door after he repeated the order, the triburst of autofire stuttering on as one sound when Bahkar roared in rage and frustration, then floored the gas. He cursed them in Arabic, his war cry spiking his ears, obliterating the rending of metal as he slammed and slashed the van through the vehicular gauntlet. He bounced in the seat, absorbing so many impacts he couldn't keep track of all the hits and scrapes and rams before he finally bulled an opening, zeroed on the plaza.

There it was! The giant sculpture, the Picasso, looming before the windshield. Was it a woman or a dog? No matter, as that, too, was seconds away from becoming twisted scrap.

He stomped the gas and saw them scattering out of his path as he raced onto the plaza, a body in a suit jacket hammering off the side, sailing away, screaming. Pigeons were squawking now, a cloud of feathers and wings taking off as he raced on, letting loose another war cry, bird bodies slamming off the windshield when—

The window blew in his face.

He felt his body lurch back, pinned to the seat, something like a hot poker instantly tearing through his upper chest. He nearly lost his grip on the steering wheel, another fist-sized hole exploding glass in his face, slivers slashing his eyes. He saw the plaza blur, spinning in eyes stung by blood, puke rising in his throat. He was toppling next, losing consciousness when his head lolled, and he saw them on top of the roof. The van was still rolling. Good! Victory, Pyrrhic or otherwise, it would be enough, giving his death meaning and glory, after all.

And he heard their screams of terror, but far away and fading fast as he slid all the way over on his side. How could he have missed them? he wondered. They were waiting for them, but how? SWAT, FBI, it didn't matter, they were deadly black wraiths in the mist, high above, silent bullets tearing into his torso, chewing him up, thrashing him.

Rolling still, a mental picture of the lobby doors framed but fuzzy in his head. He felt his thumb on the activating button. He willed his thumb to move, go down, then the lights snapped off.

NO STRANGER to Chicago, Bolan knew a little something about the Merchandise Mart. Second only to the Pentagon in square feet, it demanded an entire block, and thirteen floors high if he counted right. A landmark to the rich and famous, and there was no doubt in the Executioner's mind the jihad butcher had his sights set on barging inside, laying waste to as many workers and shoppers as possible before torching himself. On the plus side, the place wasn't opened yet to the public, no tours, just a straggling workforce making its way in.

Bolan was up and dashing across the bridge once the glass storm blew over. The Iraqi broke into a sprint, flying off the north end of the crossover, veering for the plaza. The Executioner focused, driving top speed out of his legs, his Uzi like some baton in his fist. The soldier charged on, closing the gap, as the killer was turning. Everything else—the cries of wounded, Daley command and control squawking for him to respond, the descending rotor wash—was ignored as peripheral irritants.

The jihad jackal held back on the trigger of his assault rifle, sweeping a flying wall of steel-jacketed rounds toward the bridge. Whether he was near exhaustion or feeling a terror overload, Bolan couldn't say, but the jumping AK-47 appeared to knock the gunner back. The hood of a cab took his landing, the man kicking at the ground like some dangling spider, then rolling over the hood, coming off the cab in an ungainly landing.

It was now or never, Bolan, bringing up his Uzi, ran off the bridge. No walking wounded, no civilians at all in the vicinity, ground zero was clear and free.

The jihad killer was whirling, firing one-handed, bellowing something in Arabic the soldier couldn't make out and didn't care. The box was in his hand, thumb settling over the doomsday button when Bolan risked the line of slugs flying around the compass, bearing down. Cutting his surge down to a roll, the Executioner hit the trigger of his Uzi. The soldier's 9 mm barrage marched up the enemy's torso. Bolan raked the storm, left to right when the human missile blew.

The Executioner threw himself into a nosedive, sliding for cover on the far side of the cab as the super-heated explosion vaporized the martyr and pounded the Merchandise Mart.

THE REAPER WAS well into his adopted Mr. Cool act. Somehow fate or luck had him moving well beyond the danger zone. He was on his way but hardly home free.

It had been an impulsive decision, ditching the van not even a full block from where he'd engaged Belasko. Rage, paranoia and fear of not getting what he wanted had fueled him to throw it all away and just take his chances. Sheer tenacity and the will to kill and survive would see him through. So far, so good. He figured the Iraqis had gone for the glory somewhere up Wacker, near the bridge, and all units were focused that way.

Cool.

And he'd simply strolled on, backtracking right past the Fed wagon he'd blown to hell. Using alleys, the HK subgun was kept nestled in the war bag, zipper open to allow quick and easy access just in case there was a Fed problem, or another encounter with his primary enemy. He cursed over the uncertainty of the shoot-and-run play, not sure if he'd tagged the bastard. So much had happened so quickly, but he lived in hope that if Belasko was still among the living he'd show up again.

Professional pride on the back burner, the problem now, he knew, was getting out of the city.

Despite his immediate concern, Bowen grinned at the mayhem. The frozen legions, crouched or crying up and down the street, stares fixed north where all the racket was confined for the moment. Godzilla times twenty, he thought, had come to town, tearing down the city, squashing folks on the rampage. All things considered, the jihad strike couldn't get any better than this.

So he walked on, picking up the pace a little as he melted into a loose mob heading south. That was the way to do it, he figured, fall in, best he could, just another terrified citizen, another face in the crowd. Of course, a description of his mug had to be all over local and state and federal bans by now. They were sure to be hunting him, but the hope was that the jihad wild bunch would tie up the badges until he could figure his next move, be on his merry way to Hollywood.

Just keep watching the streets, he told himself. If Chicago's finest flew up, the SMG would come out and start blasting. No sense in pulling it back now, he'd been ready since abandoning the van to shoot his way out of town, even if it came down to some suicide Alamo grandstand.

He was feeling that way, meaner by the minute, the paranoia welling until it seemed as if his own flesh were shredding apart, hot razors tearing him up from the inside out. Like the jihad troops, he believed he was ready to go off, and it wouldn't take much to get him cranked to slaughter overdrive, even if that meant standing his ground and getting cut to ribbons by cops.

He felt alive, though, somehow rejuvenated by all the chaos around him. He decided the fear was a good thing, keeping his head clear and alert. With all the wailing and gnashing of teeth, questions being flung all over by folks who didn't have the first clue why this city was under siege, and he couldn't hold back the chuckle any longer.

Damn, but he wished he knew this town better. He used the Sears Tower, rising for the sky due south, as something of a compass point. If he recalled correctly from a very brief perusing of maps, he believed the bus terminal was somewhere south. Or, with O'Hare west, midway south...

Escape and evac was going to prove a major hassle. Ride, fly or maybe carjack a vehicle, although it looked a few abandoned wheels were already scattered about. The way it looked and sounded for the most part, motorists were now ramming their way clear through intersections, fighting, no doubt, to flee the Loop.

Every citizen for himself. Bowen liked it. Radio and TV would have sounded whatever the cop version of ThreatCon Delta by now, maybe even the Army and National Guard were on the way to seal up the town, hunt down the jihad bunch. That could mean roadblocks, checkpoints, making interstates and major avenues little more than parking lots. How would the colonel's lackeys ever find him in this hell? How would he get to L.A.? What about collecting his money?

It was a mess, all right, Armageddon everywhere he turned, but all the commotion could well provide the only means of cover to clear him out. He'd worry about Los Angeles later.

Still the horror curdled some icy joy in his guts. He might as well enjoy the show while he walked, all of it a maze of hellish noise, the panic frozen in the air like a poisoned cloud, women weeping, menfolk not knowing which way to run, what to do.

Anarchy. It was a beautiful thing, he thought.

Time-out, something felt wrong. He was giving his

rear a scan when he spotted the blue-and-whites. His heart lurched, as uniforms disgorged, but they peeled off in the opposite direction, abandoning ship. Then he looked up, ears tuning in to the rotor wash, as two choppers hovered above the towering landmarks of what had become a rampaging urban jungle. Paranoia swirled to panic, Bowen finding himself suddenly, strangely alone on the sidewalk. Unaware, he had halted, the stampede thinning out, all citizens looking to make a beeline for the Sears Tower. A black rage gripped Bowen, the snarling voice in his head telling him he was about to be hemmed in. Or was he? Choppers sailed on, but he wasn't sure of anything, and how could he know for certain they hadn't spotted him? He cursed, looked right, and went through the door of what appeared on first glance some coffee shop or diner.

"...all citizens, if you are at home, you are urged to stay there. If you are downtown and inside, you are to remain there. We are informed the doors to major businesses are about to be locked, and we have a list—"

"What's up?"

Someone hissed, "Shh!"

Bowen smiled, stepping toward the crowd, putting on a dumb act. He kept grinning through the rising hatred, a few eyes glancing his way, sizing him up, he thought, wondering. He counted heads. Fourteen in all. They were all glued to the reporter jabbering away on the TV mounted to the wall.

He wasn't sure what exactly was coming over him, but it was a heat, boiling from the center of his being as he stood there, ignored, wanting to shout. What the hell, was he the invisible man or something? He felt himself shaking, one man staring at him, then looking away.

"You all right, mister?"

"Just peachy."

He was still looking at him, then going back to the TV. Bowen had the urge to announce he was the star of the show that had them so mesmerized. He was viewed with contempt and suspicion, a nobody in their eyes when he was more somebody than they could ever imagine.

"Hey, honey," he called to the waitress. "How about a cup of coffee?"

He was treated to a flashing scowl as she waved her hand at him to be quiet. That went well, he thought. He stood there a second, the talking head babbling on how the governor of Illinois was calling in the National Guard and Army Special Forces.

Bowen looked over his shoulder. It was clear out front, spooky quiet except for the din moving farther down the block, sirens shrieking in the distance, but who could tell where they were or coming from? He was thinking he probably wouldn't make it out of the city, after all, never get his hands on all that cash he had worked so hard for. No retirement, no paradise, then. All for nothing. Life could suck that way, he guessed, man should never plan anything more than the day ahead. He was thinking how much he really detested the human race. Always wanting, demanding, never giving, like this bunch, he thought, acting as if they deserved something because they simply existed when they should be bowing and scraping before him. Man, he could really use a few cold beers about now, some white powder, too, to get him right, steady the shakes, but no score there, either. He settled the bag on a table and delved inside. It took a few moments, nobody paying attention, but he threaded the sound suppressor to the subgun. Two fresh wrapped clips were already good to go. This was a freebie, he decided, something to keep him motivated.

He pulled out the SMG and took care of the TV first with a 3-round attention getter. He damn near laughed at the shock and horror paralyzing them. They wouldn't sit still long, and they were jumping to their feet next, howling, slamming into each other when Bowen let it rip. He zipped the cook and the waitress first, since they were closest to the kitchen, the only exit he could find other than his stand to block the front door. Left to right and back, raking sprays of subgun fire mowing them down, tangled limbs, shredded heaps tumbling all over the place, crimson scarecrows flopping down into booths. After the last round Bowen had the works pulled, fresh mag flipped around, cocked and was firing on as the walking wounded scrambled behind the counter. Where the hell did they think they could go anyway? he wondered. And the Reaper edged forward, the second barrage nailing them point-blank, bodies crashing through display glass, doughnuts chewed by a wild round or two. An old man was falling back, hands held out as if that would save him. Bowen helped him land with a burst to the chest.

When it was over, he found himself briefly amazed, even slightly disappointed at how quick and easy it went. All of them, shipped off to the beyond in about the time it would have taken him to chug down two cold ones.

No fuss, no muss.

He listened to the silence, grinning. No sirens on the way that he could tell, no cops on the charge. They were busy somewhere else.

He admired the carnage.

He crunched back through glass, retrieved his bag and stowed the SMG. He was alone. He could sense the street. It seemed no one was aware of his sideshow. He was moving behind the counter when he spotted the pen and pad by the cash register.

"What the hell, why not."

It felt so easy, his instinct was laughing back, telling him he might get out of town, unmolested, after all. He left the note on the counter, read it back.

To Belasko

Sorry about the mess here. Better luck next time. Nice trench coat, by the way. Maybe I'll catch you out in Hollyweird.

He nodded several times, watching the street, nothing coming his way.

Good to exit.

The Reaper turned and pushed through the door.

10

The magnificent mile.

And this was no walk-through, he thought, checking it out, envisioning the moment, drawing a mental map of the strategy. Between the Chicago River and Oak Street, it was everything Gabil al-Salidin could have hoped for and then some. Big buildings. Big money. Fancy hotels.

Big crowds.

A mile of death within the next few moments. Their fabled Gold Coast was due north, he believed, the enclave of still more obscenely rich. There was ostentatious Streeterville to the east, then the Navy Pier, all manner of targets out and about in the parks along Lake Michigan. If he was blessed with good fortune, he would make it up to the Gold Coast or maybe the shoreline, slaughtering on, the bloodied and broken bodies strewn in his path, slain by a holy warrior who would never have dreamed such a moment as this possible before now.

To strike their blow for jihad, though, on North Michigan Avenue, he thought, the very showpiece of

American wealth, would signal not even the rich could buy safety.

Or their lives.

So many targets, he thought, as Salidin disgorged from the van after Muammar crossed the Michigan Avenue Bridge, and he couldn't quite decide where to begin. The low-rise building to the west, headquarters for the *Chicago Sun-Times* perhaps? The Wrigley Building? The Tribune Tower? Saks? FAO Schwarz? Loyola University? Marshall Fields?

So many choices, so few holy warriors, so few bullets. It was maddening, trying to decide where to begin the slaughter. There had never been this sort of difficulty when gassing a Kurd village. In and out. Wholesale slaughter from the safety of a helicopter.

Never again, of course, would he get so grand an opportunity to kill so many of his hated enemies in so short a time. Salidin knew he'd never see the soil of Iraq again, wouldn't live out the coming hour, and that made his choice of targets that much harder.

Every bullet had to count.

They were hitting the sidewalk when the decision was made for them. Three, then four police cruisers were screaming over the bridge when Muammar stomped the gas, racing in reverse.

"The bus, Rabaq! With me!"

It was a brief look over his shoulder, the AK-47 out of the duffel bag, when Muammar blew up the van, a vaporizing fire cloud that consumed the cruisers, the explosion eating up nearby cars, the whole raging mass of flames and debris pounding the sidewalks. Naturally people started screaming next, as Omardh cut loose with his AKM assault rifle, a flying gnarl of arms and legs crashing through the plate glass.

Salidin held back on the trigger, moving up the bus on the street side while he heard, then saw the bodies getting scythed up where Omardh hit them from the sidewalk. The driver was attempting to bulldoze into traffic, horns blaring all over the street, sounding as one din, when Salidin broke into a sprint. They were packed inside the bus, human cattle as he viewed them, elbow to elbow, barely standing room. They screamed and shoved and ducked as Salidin blew in the windows, slicing them up before he reached the driver as he burned up the clip. He blew the driver out of his seat. Commuters were banging on the door as Salidin flipped the double mags around, cocked and went back to the slaughter, catching them as they jammed the well.

How long, he wondered, before the police swarmed over them? Ten wrapped banana clips at his disposal, he intended to go through every last round before he was martyred.

"THE MURDERING BASTARDS just opened fire on Michigan Avenue! Four—five more officers down!"

"Turn it around and get me there," Bolan ordered the chopper's pilot, the soldier squeezed into the cockpit hatch. "Drop me as close to them as possible. How many?"

"Another suicide van that way," the pilot said, keying his com-link. "Three on the loose on Michigan! Two of them are shooting up a bunch of citizens trapped on a bus!"

The police flyboys looked set to blow from their

own rage, cursing, and Bolan could damn well understand their murderous ire. Every second lost in the air, the soldier knew, cost more lives.

When they had picked Bolan up after the jihad soldier spread himself in countless pieces up and down the riverfront face of the Merchandise Mart, the Executioner fielded the situation reports from all over the city.

It was nothing short of urban apocalypse.

Two murdering SOBs had marched into the bus terminal and started shooting. Bolan had been en route to assist, the Sears Tower blurring away to the south now as the PD JetRanger swung around, vectoring north by northeast. Feeding his Uzi with a fresh clip, Bolan went to the doorway, mentally tabbing the numbers of murdering anarchists down. Two at Adams, but not before one of the human bombs went off. Bolan caught a glimpse of the mangled cars of the El train teetering on the edge of the raised track, bodies strewed across the tracks and platform. Two more nailed by his own hand. Three down at the bus terminal where Omega Two and SWAT had just lowered the boom. Two jihad men had gone berserk at O'Hare, situation not yet under control at the terminal in question. Daley Center was hit with a suicide van, four more jihad killers finally taken out by police snipers that way. Figure twenty, thirty tops, if the setup was similar to Brooklyn, and the Executioner feared they weren't even halfway home yet.

And there were reports now of looting and rioting on the South Side, random shootings, as citizens came unraveled, wondering whether or not this was the end of the world or life as they knew it in America. The ex-

pressways, Bolan saw, were parking lots. Nearly every
street leading out of the Loop was a mass exodus of
panic-driven citizens. EMT vehicles and cruisers
threaded their way through running mobs and abandoned cars to get to the wounded. Medevac and more
police choppers, used to ferry some of the SWAT
troops, crisscrossed the skyline.

It was war, Bolan knew. And they hadn't even begun
to start counting the bodies of dead civilians.

The Executioner moved back into the cockpit hatch
as the chopper descended, sailing down the glass-and-
concrete canyon of Michigan Avenue.

And Bolan took in the next urban killing field.

BOWEN WAS MOVING west on Madison Street, marching in the opposite direction from the latest batch of
blue force. The jihad show went on, at some point to
the east and south, so the Reaper hurried to catch up to
the next pack of fear-crazed citizenry. He was thinking
he needed wheels in the worst way, a carjacking most
likely when the black sedan came sliding up to the
curb. He dropped a hand over the butt of his Desert
Eagle, then froze.

He couldn't believe it. The colonel's newest man
didn't look too happy to see him, but that was understandable, considering the fact Bowen could be sure
there was a bounty on his head. The driver had the window down, jerking a nod at his pal in the back seat.

"Get in! Quickly!"

Uh-huh, Bowen thought, all's forgiven. Was this a
little too easy, or what? He had the door open and saw
the North Korean reaching inside his coat. Bowen threw

the heavy war bag in the back. The guy was grunting, scowling, still going for it when Bowen jumped in, wedging him against the door. The mammoth stainless-steel hand cannon was out in the man's ribs as Bowen slammed the door, one eye on the driver.

"Call me crazy," Bowen said, jabbing the muzzle deeper into the man's side, "but something tells me this is a little more than a coincidence. Want to tell me how you found me when this whole city's a war zone and even the cops are forced to bang their way in to get all the dead and wounded?"

The driver looked in the rear glass. "Your bag."

"And?"

"A little something was placed in there before you picked it up at the storage unit. So you wouldn't get lost."

"A homer?"

"You are very smart."

"And I don't like smart-ass," Bowen growled. "Let's roll. I'll take this, friend," he said, relieving the man of his Glock. "I heard the colonel say we have a plane to catch somewhere. He also said you were going to see that I got my money."

"Los Angeles. Once we are there," the driver said, pulling away from the curb.

"Nice and easy. I'm a little edgy right now."

"Who isn't?"

"What did I say about being a smart-ass?"

THE EXECUTIONER LEAPED from the chopper, dropped the three or four feet and hit the roof of an abandoned vehicle. There were two gunners, and wherever the third had gotten off to...

One at a time.

As the chopper flew back to the burning wreckage, searching for a suitable LZ, Bolan slung the Uzi, drew the .44 Magnum Desert Eagle. It was a long shot, that there were any survivors in that lake of fire. His senses were being stung by the clawing bite of roasted flesh and torched fuel. The Executioner set his sights on the jihad butchers, flying off the vehicle, charging on to punch their tickets. He could hear people moaning and crying inside the bus, the latest round of sirens filling his ears. Bloody arms were wedged in glass teeth, hanging down, crimson streams running down the side. Hot rage swept through Bolan, there then gone.

Down to business.

The enemy was off the walk, crossing Ohio Street, shooting up buildings beside them or firing at whoever was running, raking cars with autofire as if vandalism was simply part and parcel for their twisted cause.

The Executioner slowed up to make his own statement.

Bolan drew down, lined one up in a clear field, nothing but head in his sights, and tapped the trigger. Seeing his comrade in murder nearly decapitated, the second gunner whirled, firing his assault rifle and hollering. The Executioner loosed another burst of steel thunder, and sent the savage flying back, minus gun and sans half of his skull.

That left one. Where?

The racket of weapons fire sounded south, one block down, he believed. He backtracked, forced to ignore the commuter who tumbled out the window of the bus, the calls for help. He was rounding the corner, his tac radio squawking when he saw the small army of uniformed officers storming the lobby of the Hotel Intercontinental. Listening, he searched the carnage around him, the weapons fire petering out, dying in the next moment.

Three more down.

Bolan responded to Connors. "What do you have?"

The Executioner heard about the massacre at the coffee shop and took in the location.

"But there's something I think you might want to see," Connors told him, and Bolan wasn't sure why he didn't like the sound of that.

A SENSE OF NUMBING SHOCK had settled over the hostages. Or at least that was how Thomas Shaw read the faces around him in the passenger cabin. They were also still on the ground, and as the minutes dragged, with each screaming passover of fighter jets, Shaw felt a curious air of subdued hope but rising fear among the abductees. Another rescue attempt? If that happened...

He recalled the bodies he'd seen when boarding, maybe eight to ten dead men, heaped on the floor, one of them sitting upright where he'd been shot in the head, in the war room of the high-tech spy plane, or whatever it really was. It didn't take much analysis to deduce how their abductors had taken the superplane. It was another inside job, and it left him wondering once again how many men, in positions of power, were involved in the conspiracy. The cabin windows were shut, blinding him to what was really happening outside. Two of their guards were watching, one on each end of the aisle.

The real fear, he knew, was when the North Korean

would snap. What if the man's hand was forced and he didn't get whatever it was he demanded, which most likely was to be free to fly on? What if they were being kept from getting airborne, the North Korean stalled, various promises made to him while a commando raid was initiated on the aircraft? How many of the people sitting near him would die? His main concerns, of course, were his wife and daughter, and if armored commandos blew a hatch and stormed the craft, bullets flying, Shaw determined he'd fling his family to the floor, cover them with his own body, die in the attempt, whatever it took.

A part of him felt responsible somehow for the plight of everyone there. That wasn't true, perhaps even foolish or grandiose to believe he was that important that they had been abducted simply because this North Korean and his American counterparts wanted the Titan Four. The others...well, what? Insurance? And the very notion they were being kidnapped, American citizens abducted by their own government or intelligence operatives, forced to go to North Korea...

The Korean came into the passenger cabin, two more of the gunmen by his side. Shaw froze, reading the dark storm of rage in the man's eyes. He was pointing at a woman, barking for the troopers to take her.

Before he was aware of it, Shaw was on his feet, the words out of his mouth. "No! Take me instead!"

"Thomas..."

He ignored his wife, the colonel looking his way, deciding something.

"You're trying to leave here," Shaw said, willing away his own amazement, not sure whether the North

Korean was galled by his stand, about to lose face with this show of impertinence. "Obviously someone out there needs to be convinced. I'll help you."

The colonel was nodding, the guards looking back, paralyzed in midreach for the woman. "And you can help?"

"I can try."

"Perhaps," he said, and the silence hung. "Perhaps you can at that. I'll bring her anyway, just in case."

"Listen..."

"Take Mr. Shaw with us!"

His wife was grabbing his arm, but one of the black-clad guards was wrenching him away, shoving him ahead. Shaw saw two more men zipping open bags, hauling out blocks of a puttylike substance, trailing wires and a det cord, he believed. They began sticking the plastic explosive to the bulkhead, Shaw feeling the fear gripping him again, icy cold. That the Korean was willing to blow the plane, obviously commit suicide sent a charge of terror through the hostages, voices demanding to know what was going on, guards barking for them to be quiet.

"Should they not be convinced," Shaw heard the North Korean tell him, the woman crying out as she was jerked from her seat, "then you can watch this nice lady die."

THE FACES of official rage grew darker at each scene of mass murder. Tac radios were squawking, uniforms bustling about, voices edged with barely suppressed fury when Bolan walked into the coffee shop. Connors was putting his radio away, looking from the Executioner to the sprawled corpses and back again.

"It's on the counter," Connors told Bolan.

Bolan saw the note, picked it up and read it.

"Our bastard from the hotel, I'm thinking."

Bolan clenched his jaw, nodded. Bowen had never been far from his angry thoughts, but now it looked as if Bolan's adversary was on his way out of an urban hell he'd helped to create.

Hollywood. Spelling it out, no less, taunting him. In his face.

Bolan felt the fist of anger squeezing his guts tighter, the soldier staring at the dead. It made no sense why the man would just walk in there and starting shooting people for no reason.

Bowen was pure evil, a destroyer of life wherever he could take it. This was pretty much meant for his eyes only, Bolan reckoned. So be it. Whatever it took, the Executioner determined he would make it to Los Angeles. With the chaos fanning out to the suburbs, the resources of law enforcement stretched to their limits, Bolan figured Bowen stood a good chance of slipping through any net.

"A citizen stumbled onto this. Amazed he got through, the way 911's tied up. But I guess you can imagine."

"Your men?"

"Orson and Medly didn't make it. I think my other guy's going to lose a leg."

Bolan needed to raise Brognola, but he'd do it on the chopper ride to O'Hare. From what he'd heard, it was cleanup for the most part, National Guard and Army were on the way to restore whatever calm they could. Chicago would be locked down for days, even weeks to come. If there were still more hardmen moving about, ready to strike...

Bolan wasn't bailing, but he knew the amount of red tape hassle about to head his way. He figured he'd done all he could here.

Los Angeles, then.

Figure rush hour had started by now. No alarms sounding from the West Coast but after what he'd seen in Chicago he could well suspect yet more Iraqi time bombs were on the move out there.

He gave Connors one last look, not sure what he read in the man's eyes, other than rage over the loss of life, his own men and civilians they couldn't save.

"Get going, Agent Belasko," Connors finally said. "I know you want this bastard—I only wish I could be there. I don't know how you'll find him, but find him. If he is where he says he's going to be, nail him."

"Count on it," the Executioner said, and walked away, heading for the police chopper grounded on the street.

11

Senator Darren Sterling, Democrat from Oklahoma, believed he had a way out of his troubles. It would take subtle degrees of high finesse, wording the argument just so, spelling out the pros and cons, but it could be done. Manipulate the script when called for, such as letting her know how much he understood her own problems, indeed, felt her pain. In other words, pretty much finagle basic female emotions, a dose of compassion here, some measure of sympathy there, until she saw his side, thus naturally found herself in complete agreement there was only one way.

His way.

Of course, when all else failed, there was money, the universal language that broke down all barriers, regardless of race, religion or social stature. Whether it was some Third World backwater dump or the high-and-mighty movers and shakers of his own circle who made the laws of the land and decided which one of those impoverished Third World hellholes received a handout, money talked and the others were left wishing and wanting. Extortionists—and that's precisely what they were, blackmailing spies and con men. Most folks, he knew, could be reasoned with when money was both the problem and the solution.

This particular dilemma could be different, he realized, and hence the nagging doubt, his own persistent fear of failure. This was Su Lin he was dealing with after all.

It had been a long day already, he could use a shot or two of Dewars, and it wasn't even lunch yet. Sterling had canceled all morning appointments and begged off several meetings with colleagues. Luckily no Senate sessions or hearings were scheduled—or were there? If so, he would have been more frantic than he already was. How could he work? Su Lin was relentless, having already left a slew of messages on his e-mail, hogging his personal phone and answering machine, even ringing the line of his personal assistant off the hook until she was beginning to give him that wondering what-the-hell eye.

It went like this, every agonizing call, verbatim. "We need to talk. Immediately. I strongly urge you to fit me into your busy schedule, and this morning. I do not like being ignored." Then signing off—the wicked bitch— Mistress Su summons her slave boy. It was beyond embarrassing, way past frightening. It was personal and professional suicide; he had risked his entire world, his career for the best piece of tail.

He had practically fled his Capitol Hill office when the calls started coming in with her silken voice dripping with the sexual innuendo, switching tones to husky with implied threats.

"I won't be ignored. I will become your worst nightmare. Fool with Mama Su and you will beg to be castrated before I am done with your butt."

Enough was enough.

He had the number of her suite, and there was fifty grand in an envelope in his topcoat, more to come but only if she did a few things for him in return. Like get the hell out of town and never come back. Like have her North Korean sponsors vanish, leave him be, forget whatever his role in their scheme.

Luckily it was a fairly decent drive since the commuting crush was still concentrated getting into D.C. and not out. It felt like an endless journey but at the same time too short.

He was out of his Lexus, checking the lot, racked by paranoia and guilt. And a good amount of shame, wondering how in the world he let himself get photographed, videotaped and whatever else they had in some of the more tawdry scenarios he and Su Lin acted out. Head bent, he breezed into the lobby, not making eye contact with anyone, but glancing at the desk, grateful they were tied up with guests, too busy to take note and maybe wonder if they hadn't seen him somewhere before. He was famous in his own right, after all, making the talk-show circuit on a regular basis, Larry, Geraldo, Matthews, Russert, out there, always good for a few chuckles at the expense of his Republican counterparts, making the other side sound like bigoted idiots.

No one could save him this day, he knew, not unless he could walk on water, raise the dead, lay waste to the evil slut of his own Sodom and Gomorrah.

The truth nearly made him retch, the more he thought about it. He couldn't shake the feeling he'd been followed. He had visions of some reporter leaping out of nowhere, camera popping off and mike in his face, with Su Lin laughing and telling the whole world about their sessions.

Oh, God.

If the problem was simply money, he knew his plan would go off without a hitch. He'd paid off plenty of people in the past, those hangers-on who lived only for their fifteen minutes of fame at his expense. The ex-wife and her army of lawyers for instance, that reporter from the *Washington Post* who was on the verge of breaking the story about his brief period of cocaine use long ago. There were various and sundry sexual forays along the way other than Su Lin, of course, all of whom had been grateful to accept a fistful of cash, sans book deal, and all was well. None was as sticky or trouble-some as his North Korean situation. Thing was, *they* had been paying *him,* dumping hefty sums into off-shore accounts which they had opened in his name, in the guise of campaign contributions. Why would she take his money when they were more than likely sup-porting, financing her? He had to try. Something. Any-thing.

If it weren't for the pictures, he thought, shuddering, but grateful once again no one was waiting at the ele-vator bank. He pushed the button, stabbed it, impatient. A man in his position, well, if the truth did come out, he would be a laughingstock. He would be worse than publicly ridiculed. He cursed, scowling around, the doors opening to disgorge well-heeled men and women, full of themselves, the sort of frenetic energy, he thought, that told everybody they had money and stature but it was never enough and the little people could only ever wish to be them. He shouldered his way past the last of the bunch, hit the button, closing the doors to the muttered oath.

Alone.

What a sly trap it had been. They had found and exploited weakness. It was basic enough, though, simple moth to the flame, or the black widow gobbling up her prey in the web. Exactly what their intentions were, he couldn't say, but they wanted power, he was sure, something just as important as money, maybe even more sought after in this town. Thinking he was going to fail buying her off, he felt the panic rising. He hadn't called—he was just showing up. Maybe she'd stepped out. What if she wasn't alone? What if the saboteurs who had used her to clip his wings were in the suite? He was in too deep, though, too far gone to not do something. Another divorce settlement might unearth his secrets, not to mention grab up another hefty chunk of change. Not to mention landing him in prison. With the current administration, he couldn't see any pardon at the end of the tunnel.

The door opened, and he practically ran to her room. Something then nagged him about leaving the office so quickly. Chicago had been attacked that morning by international terrorists, so CNN had reported, and he now recalled the Senate was ordering an emergency session for all its members. Damn! Su Lin, it was her fault. She had his head so clouded with terror, but there was something else swirling around inside, causing the earlier lapse. Desire to see her, that was it, and he couldn't deny he missed her and everything they did together.

He banged on the door. He waited for what felt like

forever, scouting the hall, was about to knock on the door again when it opened. Her heady fragrance, a touch of jasmine and sweet fruit, hit him first, his voice fleeing him as she stood in the doorway. Her smile was infuriating but it was difficult, if not impossible, to keep from staring. Long raven-black hair, a taut, ivory-olive body. All the right parts, showed off beneath the flimsy white silk garment, were barely concealed by a push-up bra and some razor-thin panties.

Tall now in black pumps, she was rolling a leg, taunting him. "Oh, my little boy has come to Mama Su. This is even better than I'd hoped."

"Are you...?"

"Yes, quite alone. And lonely." A hard edge turned up in the smile. "The way you stand there, what, you think I'm some cheap working girl who would entertain gentleman friends other than Mama Su's little slave...."

He brushed past her. "We need to talk. And stop talking like that!"

"My, my, so tense."

Sterling charged around the massive living room, whirling, breathing hard, not seeing anything but Su Lin in her skimpy negligee. The woman seemed to float down the foyer, and for a moment his fear was almost evaporated by lust. That damnable smile, though, he thought, Su Lin having the world by the tail, knowing it, laughter in her eyes.

Laughing at him!

"You look like you could use a drink."

"No—yes!"

"Dewars. Two cubes, coming up, cutie boy."

Always boy, he thought. Talking down to him, no respect, never amount to a damn thing. Mama's boy, old Dad always groused, even though she'd treated him with pretty much the same contempt, which he discovered, too late, in the woman he'd stumbled across to marry the first time around. He squeezed his eyes shut, something hot and sharp, beyond anger, carving through him, bringing a roar into his ears, drowning out the voices from the past. He wished he were strong enough to simply will away the judgment and criticism in his head, but he never could, always failing, it seemed, when he needed to stand up and be counted the most.

Then he felt her fingers brush through his hair, flinching as he smelled her again, breezing past, a whiff of exquisite sin, calling him for a taste of heaven but fraught with the fires of hell at the end of the ride. He gathered his thoughts, or tried, wondering where all that brilliantly contrived dialogue he had hammered out during the drive had gone to. She was behind the wet bar, he saw, smiling, playing with her hair as she built the drink. Life was just one big, grand party for her, he thought. Men were just something to use and discard when they no longer served her needs. So why did he still want this evil slut so bad?

"We can't go on like this, Su Lin," he started, finding his voice, legs somehow taking him forward.

She laughed, that hard edge back at the corners of the smile. "Like what? Here, be a good boy and drink up. You need to relax, loosen up. Where's my party boy I know and want so much?"

He grabbed the glass, killed it before he knew it,

slammed it down. She poured him another. "Look, Su Lin, we both fell into something that was way over our heads. It was a mistake."

"Aren't they all?"

"What? What do you mean by that?"

The smile almost vanished, something dark, though, walking through her eyes. "Nothing. Go on."

He cleared his throat, took another sip for courage. "I'm not sure exactly who put you up to all this or why, but it has to stop. No more calls. No more goons circling around, showing up at my home, my office, making threats and demands, telling me what to do. Whatever you have of us, video, pictures, tape recordings, whatever, I want them back. With the negatives."

He couldn't believe what he saw. Was that compassion in her eyes? She was nodding again, looking—what? Sorry for him? Ready to give in?

She laid her hands on the bar, red fingernails like small daggers, drumming them, gaze narrowed. "And what do I get for saving you? What does Su Lin get to go away?" She made some grand flourish with her hands. "Really, now. Do you think I want to give all this up, scurry back to Pyongyang, just another filthy peasant bitch?"

"You're saying it will cost me."

"Oh, and plenty. I am not some whore you can do with as you please, then toss aside like a dirty magazine when you're done playing with yourself."

They were getting somewhere. Good. He could feel it now. The universal language was being spoken. Sterling took out the envelope, dumped it on the bar top.

"What's this?"

"Fifty thousand. It's yours."

She snorted.

"Make it all go away, as you put it, and there's more."

She took the money, slipped a nail inside, nodding. "It's been a while since you've given Mama Su anything. I was starting to think you didn't care about us." She didn't smile now as she wedged the envelope inside her panties, all business.

"So? Do we have a deal?"

"A deal?"

He studied her watching him. "You want more."

"I always want more," she said, voice silky, the eyes going smoky for a moment. "More is a good thing."

"How much?"

She turned to ice. "Millions."

"What?"

"Tens of millions. Billions."

Sterling felt his head spin. "What are you saying? What, are you crazy? You took the money just now and—"

"Shut up," she snapped. She was around the bar before he could find his voice, smiling again. Sterling felt himself paralyzed by her audacity, the venom in her tone. She started toying with his tie, tightening it, breathing on his face. He slapped her hand away, getting the picture as she put pressure on his throat. The slap came back like lightning, the crack ringing his ears, his face on fire. He shook with rage, Su Lin stepping back, out of range, laughing.

"You listen to me and you listen very good," she said.

It took him a few moments to get his senses straight, rubbing his face, fighting back the impulse to charge her.

"I own you." She laughed. "The men I work for, they own you. This isn't just about money, you fool. It's about power, it's about the future of my country." She giggled. "I have plans for us, and hey, baby, I'm sorry I hit you. I just missed you so much. Please forgive me."

"You..."

"Me what? Before you say another word I'll make you regret, you hear this, my little fool. I came from nothing—I will not return to nothing, ever. I will never be broke, hungry, alone and disrespected again. Never! Now, listen to me! Maybe I really do enjoy your company sometimes. Maybe I need you, maybe we need each other. You don't know that, you don't know how I really feel, and you never will, either."

Sterling heard the roar in his ears, stronger now, a pulsating pressure. It had always been like this, he thought, and the hatred grew the more she talked. He was hearing voices from the past again. His father's voice, that two-fisted, boozing, womanizing titan among men, telling him what it was like to be a man, that he'd better show some backbone along the way or the world would eat him up. He heard Su Lin's voice, breaking through the ringing crash, her laughter thrown in his face.

"You see, you played, now it's time to pay. I have my own dreams, and letting you just pay me off and walk out the door doesn't fit into them. You will, however, start giving me a generous allowance. Fifty thousand a month should work out nicely—cash in an envelope. If Mistress Su needs more you'll be the first to know, I promise, baby."

He felt his head slumping, limbs shaking. He was stuck, trapped.

"Listen to me! Here is how it's going to be from now on. You will do as you're told, when you are told. You want to know something else about Su Lin's future with you? Someday your Su Lin will be the First Lady. But you, of course, will address me as First Mistress Su, bitch goddess of the United States of America."

"You're insane."

"No, I'm in the driver's seat."

"Just like that, I'll be President of the United States if I go along..."

"Yes. Just like that. Everyone gets what they want."

"You seem to be conveniently forgetting one detail. My wife."

"A small and insignificant problem. There will be an accident regarding her, very soon. Such things can be arranged."

She was turning away, at the end of the bar, looked to be reaching for his drink, then she laughed, a belly ripper that went on and on, swelling him with fierce hatred of her, himself—his entire life. She had it all figured out. He was a puppet. She was in charge of his life, owned his soul, even though the real power lurked in the shadows.

And it happened. He wasn't sure he'd even done it until he saw her falling, until it was too late. It couldn't have been him, but it was. It was so fast, but it seemed as if he saw the whole thing in slow motion, something he knew he'd see every day in his mind for the rest of his life. The open hand—how?—flying down, slamming her so hard in the side of the face her head seemed to snap all the way around. Only the head was going down like a great falling rock, the legs flying out from under her, her face like some frozen, lifeless caricature, a grotesque cartoon thing. Then the sickening crack as the front side of her skull ricocheted off the edge of the bar. He saw it all, paralyzed, replaying what he'd just done, staring at his hand next, then the pointed edge of the wet bar. Her blank stare, looking up, her body sprawled on the carpet, limbs folded as if they were nothing but rubber extensions.

He heard himself blubbering now, bile in his throat as he shuddered and dropped to his knees, calling her name, over and over. "Oh, God, oh, God." He shook her, feeling around her neck, wrists. Nothing. Then he heard two voices, floating through his cries, coming to him from a great distance.

"This is not good, Mr. Kim."

"No, this is not good at all, Mr. John."

"Major damage control."

"Indeed. Major."

"Did you get it all?"

"I will make several copies shortly."

Sterling whirled, saw them slowly coming toward him, down the hall from the bedroom. Two of them, and he knew right away what they were. One North Korean in a dark topcoat and a black flattop. An American in a black leather trench coat, a white buzz cut, the same sort of cold blue eyes he'd seen on the man who'd invaded his home in Oklahoma to remind him he was bought and sold. Sterling wanted to weep. He stared back at Su Lin, as if he could will her back to life. She had lied to him again, he thought. If she had told him the truth, that they weren't alone, this would have never happened. It was her fault she was dead. The bitch!

"I didn't mean to do it! I didn't mean to kill her!"

He was bleating his pleas at them, swearing, rising.

"Sit down on the couch, Senator. And stop taking the Lord's name in vain."

"Wh-what?"

The American slapped him in the back of the head, repeating himself. "Do what I just told you."

The North Korean said, "Get control of yourself. This is a mess, a big one, we agree. But we will clean it up for you."

"You what? You w-will? How?"

He found the couch, toppled back, saw the American bringing him his drink.

"Anyone see you come in?"

"No."

"Didn't go to the desk?"

"No. I—I already knew the room."

"Elevator?"

"No."

"Did you tell anyone you were coming here?"

Sterling shook his head. "No one knows. No one."

"We will help, then," the North Korean said.

Sterling was drinking, talking to himself. How did this happen? What was he going to do?

Again his face was struck, the American slapping him a few more times until Sterling thought he would scream, glass flying, a spray of Dewars to the coat.

"Pull yourself together, Senator. We said we'd take care of it. We don't talk just to hear our own voices."

"Su Lin...but Su L-lin..."

"She was just a whore. There will be other whores for you when you are in better shape."

Sterling couldn't believe what he was hearing, but there was a sudden meanness to the North Korean's voice. The American glanced over his shoulder, smiled back in his face. "You'll have to excuse my friend's lack of sensitivity. He's not real keen on interracial nonsense. It's an alpha male pride thing. You do know something about pride, don't you, Darren?"

Sterling felt the anger coming back, then the look was slapped off his face. "Here's how it is, Darren. You just gained two new friends. One of them—that's me—will call you later at your office. Proceed with the day's business, put this behind you, forget it ever happened. Like I said, we're your friends, we know you didn't mean to kill your whore. You will meet me at a bar-restaurant, nice quiet little place in McClean I go to for happy hour. We'll get a little more chummy over some cocktails. You'll get the particulars when I call. To use your vernacular, let me be perfectly frank. You came here to weasel out. There is no way out, Darren. You want power, you want glory, you want the brass ring. If you understand me, Darren, and are willing to do whatever you are told, whenever we tell you, I want a simple nod of your head."

Sterling knew enough to understand the moment. If he pushed for his initial business here, even hinted he might hedge later on, he'd go wherever Su Lin would end up. The American straightened up, took a step back, waiting. Sterling nodded.

"Good. We understand each other. You're free to leave. I'll be in touch. I suggest you answer my calls right away."

It was a nightmare, all of it, and Sterling couldn't

move at first, then the American—his so-called new friend—looked at him, ice in his eyes. Sterling rose, couldn't bear to even glance back at Su Lin, and found himself practically running for his exit.

COLONEL CHONGJIN HAD violated one of his own iron-clad principles. He had underestimated the opposition. Sometimes sheer will, pure tenacity wasn't enough. Sometimes, like now, the other side would prove themselves capable of matching willpower. A mistake, perhaps proving a fatal miscalculation, but Chongjin was prepared to end it all on the runway, going down—or up, rather—with the ship. He would have the last say, the final laugh.

Willpower.

They hadn't moved off the runway. He scanned the skies through the cockpit portals, a blue sheet that was rapidly close to burning to a blinding glow as the sun rose higher over the desert. There was a gunship to the north, but no fighter jets now, and he found that even more disturbing. He looked at his watch again. Three minutes late, but he would give it two, maybe three more minutes. The delay would alter their own schedule once—if—they were airborne over the Pacific. That could be corrected with one radio call. He wouldn't give up, not yet, believing the American military wouldn't just let him sacrifice their own people, blow up a multi-billion dollar superplane. They would cave. They had to.

He looked at Temple, the major still scowling at the armada of vehicles, the army of lawmen and soldiers blocking the runway. The GlobeSpecter's engines were now powered up, Temple appearing to grow more concerned and anxious to get it rolling, but keeping silent, waiting it out. He was a professional at least, Chongjin thought, but he was also far too greedy for his own good.

One problem at a time.

Chongjin turned, looked at Shaw and the woman. Likewise he had underestimated the hostages. The woman, brunette, perhaps forty, was holding up, not falling apart and begging for her life to be spared as he had anticipated she would. There was a subtle change in Shaw's eyes also. When he could, Chongjin had observed his trophy. He had expected the man to grovel, demand release, issue pleas for his family to be set free. Instead, each time he looked at the scientist there was something growing in the eyes, a smoldering fire of a determination to see this through, perhaps even something else more oriented toward action. And now Shaw was the one, understanding his own importance while coming to terms with his predicament, who threw off a sense that he held one or two good cards.

He did, indeed, and it was a fine line Chongjin knew he had to walk.

Chongjin addressed the woman. "What is your name?"

She stood there, unblinking at the gunmen surrounding her. "Janet Miles."

"What are you?"

"If you mean what's my job classification, I'm an advanced technical assistant for booster refinement and laser-guided sensors on—on kill vehicles."

Chongjin found himself impressed. "Interceptor missiles."

"Yes."

"It is just you on board?"

"Yes. My son—your people took him from me back at the compound."

"I see. I regret that had to be done."

"I find that a little hard to believe."

Chongjin balked, then smiled. "You are very brave."

"I am very scared."

"That is understandable." He controlled himself, even though he was angry he couldn't break her. "You aren't afraid to die, then, if I don't hear what I want?"

"My only regret is that I'd never see my son again. You'll do whatever it is you are going to do. I'm powerless."

"You're far more powerful in your courage than you give yourself credit for being. If I have to kill you, I won't enjoy doing it."

"You don't have to do this," Shaw said. "Let me talk to whoever..."

"Mr. Shaw, please. I was merely making conversation to pass the time. They are late, but I'm being generous to a fault in my patience. Should the need arise for further convincing, I'll let you first attempt to make them see they can do nothing but obey me. Should that fail, then I'll be forced to shoot Ms. Miles."

The radio console crackled, "This is Captain Barker, Ranger White One-Five-Seven to Mother Ship One. Come in."

Chongjin punched on. "Yes, Captain Barker. The verdict?"

"You have been cleared for takeoff. Proceed."

Chongjin watched, soldiers and police falling into their vehicles, the blockade sliding in different directions off the runway.

"Listen to me very carefully, Captain Barker. I am in command and control of the most sophisticated high-tech radar and surveillance equipment your country has ever produced. You know the range on my screens to monitor air traffic, even satellite surveillance. Consult Nellis if you think I can be fooled into thinking we won't be watched. This aircraft has been mined with explosives. I won't hesitate to destroy it, perhaps even plunge it into one of your cities."

"Understood. So, what are you waiting for?"

Chongjin punched the button, ordered Temple to get them out of there. "Take her back to her seat," he told Wallace. "Mr. Shaw, you will remain with me. Once we are safely on our way, I will have your colleagues brought up. It is about time we all discussed the future."

Shaw said nothing, and Chongjin studied the man, spotting that look again. What was he thinking? Shaw, he knew, was no warrior, none of the hostages were, but they were fighters.

The colonel broke his stare, watched over Temple's shoulder as they rolled faster down the runway, thundering past what he knew was a vast, angry mob of spectators. They had their orders, and Chongjin didn't care if they came down from their President himself. The opposition was helpless, and he was on the way.

The simple pleasure of having won yet another round nearly brought the smile back.

12

The Executioner couldn't believe what he heard, pacing near the sat-link modem, Brognola's latest round of grim news seeming to hover in the Gulfstream's cabin, a living, taunting force. Not even two minutes in the air, putting behind the firestorm that was Chicago, and Bolan was forced to take another roundhouse on the jaw from the opposition.

"I guess I'm not as up on my cutting-edge technology as I should be, Hal, but you made it sound like this GlobeSpecter is damn near invisible."

"Let's just say it's real, it works, and there's only a handful of people in this town who even know of its existence. Hell, I had to hear about it from the President himself—that was when he was able to tear a few private moments away from his national-security advisers, the Joint Chiefs and all the Pentagon brass swarming the situation room over there, burning his ear about how to proceed. Classic cluster-F, everybody wants in on the act, and the Man is ducking any number of political grenades now getting hurled his way."

"But we're still in the game?"

"Our show—for now—at least on our own turf."

For now, Bolan thought. "We have what, two hundred working spacecraft out there and they can't track this superplane?"

"One hundred and eighty at last count, and I'm told not even NORAD or NASA can one hundred percent zero in on the supercraft. Sensors, radar altimeter, radiotelemetry, the whole nine yards of spy eyes from outer space, latitude becomes longitude, up is down, a fat malfunctioning AFU they lock on, but it turns out they're watching the Andes in Peru or a shot of San Diego beachfront. I don't have the specs on the thing, and the Farm can't figure out how it does what it does beyond some educated guesswork. Only thing I'm told to compare it to...well, imagine trying to film a big flying pane of glass."

"And we just let them go on their merry murdering way."

"It was a tough call, across the board, but it was the Man's directive to let them fly on."

"That much...okay, that I can maybe understand."

"Up to a point?"

"This Colonel Chongjin, he and his Phoenix Council had it all figured out. They're kicking us in the teeth all over the place, and I haven't heard how many dead and dying American citizens I left behind."

"Enough—one's enough—so that there will be flak aplenty flying all over this town for months to come, however this whole damn mess plays out. Look, as far as our call to arms went, if you're kicking yourself, don't. How it happened was something neither one of us could have prevented, not the FBI, the NSA, nobody, unless we were tipped off well advance, which wasn't about to happen. Let me tell you something, Striker, the treasonous bastards behind this, when they are dragged out of the shadows, are going down so far and so hard they might miss hell altogether on the way out. They will see capital punishment, no deals, no immunity, that's straight from the Oval Office. Now, the Man says for you to keep calling the shots as you see necessary when you hit L.A., whatever it takes, the gloves stay off."

"They're headed for North Korea, Hal."

"Well, that superplane hits North Korean airspace, Kim Jong Il can say goodbye to a lot of things, starting with his balls."

"Any ideas on where it goes next from the White House?"

"I'm not sure at this point. One strategy already fell through into the void. The plan was in the works, albeit short-lived, to stall Chongjin, keep them grounded until a Delta Team went through the hatch. The JCS practically shoved it down the Man's throat, but he canceled out."

"They mined this superplane, you said."

"Stem to stern, we think, and nobody's doubting Colonel Chongjin's willingness to push the button. So, the guys at the top here didn't want to see more Americans go up in flames again."

"Top talent, you mean, million-dollar investments for SDI, something I was led to believe was decades off from being little more than Star Trek fantasy. Now they've hijacked a one-of-a-kind superbird, and I'm sure the Washington power brokers don't want to risk the first scratch on their pet project."

"No one's going to call you Mr. Cynical on this one,

but that's a fairly accurate assessment. What we can do is use ground-based radar. Once they fly over California, we can start locking in from the ground. Hawaii next if they fly the way we anticipate, and I'm thinking once Chongjin and company think they're safely en route over the Pacific, we can scramble a few fighters out that way, monitor the plane from a distance so the bastards don't pull the plug in midair." He paused, Bolan still pacing. "It's a safe bet this superplane was hijacked, an inside job. Again, more traitors, the whole snatch from Shaw on down has been a massive coordinated effort. Nellis is right now under a full Pentagon invasion, DOD is scrambling for cover, aware they've got a lot of answering to do. I hear silence, Striker."

"Thinking ahead."

"Why am I hearing the blackest of all black ops?"

"Then we're on the same page. North Korea, basically, has declared war on this country, Hal. Iraq could use a taste of some of the horror they dished out, but I'll start with Chongjin."

"After Bowen?"

"After Bowen."

"I agree this one's headed across the Pacific, but if you're thinking what I think..."

"Where's Grimaldi?" Bolan asked, referring to his longtime friend and Stony Man's ace pilot.

"Funny you should mention old Jack. He called in. He was on R and R when I filled him in, but he's on the way back from Miami."

Any other time and Bolan would wonder out loud what the hell was with Jack and Miami these days. At least they knew where to find him.

"Have him meet me in L.A as soon as possible. We'll figure out the aircraft we'll use once we know where they touch down."

"I'll ship him your way pronto. Jack sounded a little rough around the edges...."

Bolan smiled. "Let me think on this while I'm on the way to LAX. Possible you can corral the Man and start hammering out a strategy to get us into North Korea, make it clear while you're at it this won't be any diplomatic mission."

"I'll run it by him, but..."

"L.A. first, understood."

"So far, it's too damn quiet out there. By now rush hour is nearly over, but I don't know why that makes me nervous...hold on a minute, something just came across my desk."

While Bolan waited he felt caged, shackled by the hiatus, a time bomb looking to go off in his own right, only set to blow among the ranks of the enemy and not in packed crowds of innocent civilians. Which made Bolan's blood turn to fire, as he thought about the murderous SOB, Bowen. He saw the bodies, all the blood of the innocent in that coffee shop. People just going about their own business, living their lives, another day. And then something straight out of hell comes in and just starts snuffing them out. How many widows? How many families left now without a mother, father? It was a message, sure, Bowen getting his kicks, leaving his signature, come and get me.

Bowen wanted to strike up the band again. The next dance, though, Bolan would name the tune.

"Hey, we caught a wave, Striker. The Lebanese taverna from Brooklyn?"

Bolan briefly thought back to the terrorist stash house where it had all started for him. "Yeah?"

"My people turned up a little black book full of numbers. One of them was traced down to a storage business. U-Store-It in Queens. Run, allegedly, by a South Korean family, only my guys go there and the supposed owners are nowhere to be found. Looks like their apartment was vacated, too, in haste."

"You're telling me this U-Store-It was a stash house for weapons, explosives?"

"You got it. We found a small cache in one of the bins. Now, U-Store-It is a small chain, launched, according to tax returns, roughly eighteen months ago. Three altogether. One in Chicago..."

"And one in L.A."

"My guys just grabbed a Mr. Jong at his U-Store-It in Long Beach. One of Jong's associates on the premises was more heavily armed than the Terminator. My guys took care of him, but Jong decided he still likes breathing. No going out with a roar for him."

"Let me guess. He's a simple businessman, come to America in search of a better life, has no idea why his storage bins became ammunition depots for Iraqi terrorists."

"Clueless. They're sitting on him, on my orders, waiting for you to get there to put a few choice questions to Jong. It gets better. Some concerned citizen called in to report suspicious activity yesterday, telling the FBI he thought there were terrorists in his apartment complex in Anaheim. He had no evidence. We figure the guy was thinking L.A. was set to go the way of New York and Chicago and this citizen was doing a little profiling. So I sent a team to stake the place. Lo and behold, one Muhmad al-Duahbi, Egyptian passport, is taking a stroll this morning, large duffel bag, checking my team over his shoulder. They approached, he ran, they took him down and cuffed him. They opened the bag and they were looking at ten grenades, AK-74 and enough clips to take out a city block."

"I've got an idea, Hal."

And Bolan spelled out his next move.

"Do it," the big Fed said. "I'll get it started on my end."

"That was a quote from the President, right? 'Whatever it takes.'"

"Word for word."

BOWEN FINISHED slicing up their topcoats with the commando dagger, binding the thicker strips around their wrists. The two Koreans were laid out on the carpet on their stomachs, necks craning to give him the evil eye.

"Don't go anywhere, girls." Bowen laughed, and covered the few short steps to the cockpit hatchway. There, he wedged the door open, jamming wadded-up cashmere between door and frame. The pilot, a muscular blond flight jockey, was looking over his shoulder.

"Just stick with the program," Bowen told the pilot, or you'll be the first one I pop. We clear?"

"Hey, who needs trouble? I'm just paid to fly their plane. Believe me, I want you gone every bit as bad as you want to get to L.A."

"The sushi brass doesn't pay you enough, that it?"

"Not for you to stand there waving a gun around in my face."

Bowen realized he was gripping the Browning, sound suppressor in place. He stowed it in shoulder leather, thinking it was time to help himself to the wet bar, then start digging out some straight answers from the Koreans. The more he thought about it, the more he regretted not having waxed the ground crew at the small private airfield. Three guys, in the office, telling the Korean their VIP jet was topped out with fuel, all systems go. They had acted like the three monkeys, see no evil and like that, but Bowen still figured he should have left no loose ends there. Had he killed them, though, it would have made the pilot more nervous than he already was, thinking his own ticket would get punched at the end of the ride. He was right, Bowen knew. Once they landed, the North Koreans having told him there would be a vehicle waiting for them, the pilot was history.

"Just take it easy, cowboy," Bowen told him, watching the sea of clouds as the VIP jet sailed on. This particular jet looked built for speed, Bowen asking and having been informed it could max out at a little over seven hundred miles per hour. Wheels down in sunny southern California soon. "Everything goes off, no fuss, I'll leave you tied up. By the time somebody comes looking, I'll be long gone."

The pilot sat there, silent, and Bowen could tell the flying cowboy wasn't buying it.

Quickly Bowen went and built a heavy Wild Turkey and ginger. He looked at the glass, the bottle, then killed the drink. He took the bottle, feeling better, smoothed out inside and ready to kick ass and take names, and claimed a seat beside the North Koreans, able to keep an eye on the cockpit.

"Okay," he said, crossing his legs. "Tell me how, when and where I'm going to get my half million."

They looked each other, nothing but a couple of roped slugs to Bowen. Neither looked inclined to talk.

The Reaper was out of his seat, planted his heel on the back of one's neck. "I see you need some convincing," he growled, grinding the North Korean's face into the carpet, hitting him in the eyes and gaping mouth with a Wild Turkey shower. "I only need one of you. And I hate wasting good booze on your sorry sushi ass, so one of you little fucks better start giving me some answers."

He removed his foot, the man sputtering and gagging, "Okay, okay," and Bowen reclaimed his seat.

"North Hollywood."

"What about it?"

"The money is there, cash. Funds that were used to help finance the operation. It's a studio complex. We have our man there, he makes films for foreign investors in Asia."

"I'm supposed to believe that shit? Telling me the colonel's in the movie business?"

"It's true."

"What kind of movies?"

"Adult."

Bowen felt the grin coming on. "Colonel's making dirty movies, what do you know. Go on."

"It's a front."

"No shit. For what?"

"We bring in immigrants, women, from North Korea, Philippines, Cambodia, Vietnam."

"Sex slaves, you mean? The extortion bait to reel in some of the playboys in the Phoenix Council."

"Whatever," the Korean growled.

"Don't get smart on me, asshole. And don't ad-lib. Who's in charge of this show biz?"

"His name is Bu Jin."

Bowen drank, chuckled. "Mr. Bu-Jingles, I like it. Porn entrepreneur. This is getting better all the time. So the place is actually a stash house for cash, guns and girls. Right?"

"Yes."

"And my money's there?"

"There is a large surplus of cash."

"How large?"

"We couldn't say, exactly."

"Can't or won't? Think hard before you start laying the bullshit on me."

"I have heard as much as five million."

Bowen whistled, thinking major-league fat bonus for all his time and trouble. He rethought his original plan, recharting the next leg. Offer the pilot fifty grand in cash to stay put, then get him out of the country when he came back from Hollywood. Naturally, once he was far away the pilot could be eliminated as a hanging loose end. Sorry about that, Bowen would tell him, taking back the fifty large, nothing personal. No way now, if they were telling him the truth, would he pocket a paltry half million. He wanted all of it.

Bowen sucked from the bottle, nodding and smiling. Whoever said life was tough? Naturally there was risk, lots of it, more killing when he hit the studio. Well, he'd already walked through some wildfires. He hadn't been burned yet. But, hey, he was the Reaper.

"Okay, girls," Bowen told them, "when we hit Hollywood here's the deal...."

RUPERT HADLEY WAS sick and tired of being sick and tired. Thirty-five years was a long time to be a nobody, another cowboy in the sticks, going nowhere fast, when all his life he had always figured he was destined for greatness and glory. He was different, or so he'd wanted to believe. But lately he came to realize he had to do more to find his niche in the world than sit around, get drunk around the clock, wishing and dreaming for something to happen.

Maybe something along those lines was about to happen, somebody out there aware he was an action kind of guy, after all, a stand-up act who just needed a little encouragement. Sure, somebody at least must know that he knew a little something about life on the edge. Up until then he wondered why nobody else but him saw the promise of a star, a man among men in their presence? And now, after all these years, it sounded as if somebody was coming to take him away. If that was true he would leave all the drudgery of the old life behind. Easy as hosing crap off the bottom of his shoes.

And that, he decided, was what his life had been.

Crap.

Three years was likewise another eternity, he thought, to stay henpecked by a woman who had a mouth that would make Satan wince, and telling her to go jump would simply pile the frosting on the cake a little higher and sweeter. The list of what he was sick and tired of was long and bitter, and he usually reviewed it at least once a day after tying on a load of Jack Daniel's, figuring if he drank enough he could drown out her voice, for one thing. Fat chance, since she went on the warpath whenever he tried to launch a little one-man party, ruining his buzz so bad he'd have to risk violating his parole by driving into town to drink the night away with the boys. Tired, too, of this two-story outhouse in the Rocky Mountain boondocks for starters, but it was her place—husband number three long since heading for greener pastures—even if it was a pigsty. Janie always claimed she was too damn tired from working a real job as a barmaid. He was tired, too, of dealing meth, since he could never be sure when one of the boys would get popped and start squealing, thus sending him back to prison. He was a two-timer loser, ten years altogether in the big house, something, naturally, she always reminded him about, as if it were a weapon to threaten him with, since the telephone was her favorite friend—911—whenever he popped her in the mouth after simply being unable to endure her railing. Luckily every time the sheriff came knocking he could show off a few welts and dings where she'd torn into him first, thus leaving the sheriff and his deputy shaking heads and shuffling back to the cruiser, cussing both of them.

Time to fly.

No, life was not the grand adventure he'd always dreamed of. But that was about to change, any minute now, in fact, as he stared out the window to the front yard.

This, he thought, was the first day of the rest of his life.

He took a sip of coffee spiked with Jack, searching the thick woods, the dirt trail that wound down through the high country, mentally urging them—whoever they were—to show up. A check of his watch, and they should have been there by now, as promised in yesterday's letter.

Hadley gave a search of the living room over his shoulder, listening to the silence of the house. She was still asleep, thank God, coming home, he figured, sometime late after her shift, but he'd already passed out by the time she charged into the bedroom, only somehow she still managed to fill his dreams with muttered oaths and character assassination. He strained to look down the porch, spotting the tail end of her Ford pickup, parked next to his Jeep Cherokee, just to make sure she was under the roof. It was getting harder these days to remember things, all sorts of missing time, and he had to think hard anymore to recall the past hour. He had to admit he didn't feel too shabby that morning, though, not the usual paralyzing hangover that kept him bedridden until soap time. Had to be the excitement of knowing he was about to begin anew that was funneling the sludge out of his limbs.

But what if it was some Internet clown's idea of a bad joke? A scam to get his money? Worse, a setup by Feds? That was what the 9 mm Glock, holstered beneath his nylon field jacket, was for. He also had another small arsenal in the den, just in case a cavalry of armored government goons hit the house. Folks tended not to trust Uncle Sam or his army of thugs from the FBI or Justice Department in these parts, but he understood and appreciated that sort of healthy paranoia.

The letters, though, had looked real enough, but with computers these days anything was possible. There was the Department of Defense letterhead, which had thrown him for a loop the first time. He thought they'd had the wrong guy, since the closest he'd ever gotten to anything military was a *Soldier of Fortune* convention. But the letters had been addressed to him, only strange how he was to mail the correspondence to a P.O. box in Los Angeles when DOD was way back east in the District of Clowns. Whatever. They seemed to know every detail about his life, which at first had rocketed his paranoia off the scales. But they weren't interested in his past follies and failures, nor his present lifestyle, as they put it. They only wished to know if he had a willingness to train and reshape and remold himself into the image of a warrior. They talked about personal glory. They talked about how America was going to hell but a new day was dawning when a few righteous men would rise from the ashes to take the land back. They mentioned he would have to leave the United States for a while, sweetening the pot for him still more. The big thing, the clincher, they promised a fat wad of money. Five grand up front, cash, which he could sorely use since drinking and drugs always ate up whatever he made through dealing. They always told him to destroy the letters once he read them, but he'd kept them squirreled deep beneath the other mess, the old bills, dirty magazines in his desk. He'd even transcribed them to disk, just in case she went tearing through his personal stuff, always on the hunt for more ammunition to fire off at what she wrongly considered his worthless character.

"Come on, come on, where are you?"

He found himself more ready and willing to go with them to wherever as the minutes crawled. Any place but there. To be anybody other than what he was. He felt clean and proud in his black BDUs, the black steel-tipped combat boots laced and polished even, the whole getup courtesy of a *Soldier of Fortune* catalog. He heard something then and jolted. An engine purring, coming up the drive. It was hard to focus since his brain was still fogged and throbbing from whiskey. He was smiling, chugging down the coffee, flipping the cup on her couch when he took in either his saviors or another nightmare. It was a black GMC with U.S. government plates pulling in. Two guys. He felt more paranoia flare up, but that was only natural. He'd never met them, and he couldn't quite trust the moment until he knew for sure they were on the level.

They got out. Big guys, buzz cuts, dressed in black. Something out of *X-Files,* he thought. He went to the front door and opened it.

"You Hadley?"

"In the flesh."

They looked at each other, then one said, "You ready to go?"

"Yes, sir. Can you answer a few questions first?"

"We spelled it out already. From this moment on, it's strictly need-to-know."

"Yeah, but..."

"We come in for a second?"

Hadley felt his heart lurch, peering into their cold eyes. "Yeah, sure. What's up?"

They were in, Hadley backing up when—

"What the hell's going on here?" Janie demanded.

Hadley nearly jumped a foot off the ground, her hen squall slicing razors through the pulsing ooze in his skull.

"That's what we needed to talk to you about, Hadley."

"Remember when we told you that you might be asked to prove yourself to us first? Sort of an acid test?"

"I don't know," the other man in black said. "It will take a week alone just to wring this one out. I like the Section Eights better."

"I understand. We're not running a detox. Let's see what he does."

Weird, he thought, how they talked, glancing from Janie back to him, as if neither one of them were even in the room.

"Hey, I'm talking to you, Rupert! This is my house, in case you've forgotten! What gives here, these two don't look like your usual low-life drug buddies! They look like cops, they..."

And so on, until he felt himself trembling with rage and embarrassment.

Hadley saw the first man point at the weapon beneath his jacket, nodding at Janie. Hadley's heart jackhammered. This was it; they wanted proof that he was the man they were looking for. He felt the smile, his head bobbing, the Glock seeming to fly up in his hand.

"Hey, I'm talking to you!"

He shot her in the face, fascinated for a second at how hard and fast she dropped. The silence was bliss, too.

"There's one more in the house."

Hadley whirled at the grim faces. "What?"

"There's a tan Oldsmobile out front. Only supposed to be two vehicles here."

Hadley cursed. She did that a lot lately, bringing home a girlfriend from work. The vehicle in question would be Stacey's. She'd been coming there, three or four times a week, having problems with her old man, she claimed, sleeping in the guest room after, of course, she'd helped herself to his booze. But Hadley knew Janie had her stay over to help her keep an eye on him, back up any stories of a domestic incident for the sheriff. He heard the pounding of feet, somehow got his legs moving, flying through the living room. He was bringing up the Glock, but she was already out the back door. He fired, but missed bad, the MIBs muttering curses behind him.

"Forget her. We need to go."

Hadley cursed again. He turned, shrugging, afraid they would abandon him, blame him that she was getting away.

"Move it out."

And Hadley moved, out the front door, the first man telling him to take the front seat. He was scared, thinking this was all too good to be true. As they piled in, the man fired up the engine, whipping the vehicle around. It was too late now to bail, he knew. He'd proved his mettle, a murder rap, no less, hung over his head. He was already gone, for better or worse, in search of a new life.

He sat back, thinking if this was a bust he'd already be cuffed.

"Relax, Hadley," the second man told him from behind. "We're not cops. And if we wanted you dead, you wouldn't have made it to that seat. We're here to give you a new lease on life. Are we clear?"

"Works for me," Hadley said.

"We figured as much."

13

What Bolan had lined up for the two of them wouldn't be found in any law-enforcement manual on interrogation techniques. It boiled down to terrorists out there murdering innocent American civilians, blowing up what amounted to whole city blocks and threatening to spiral the democratic way of life, liberty and the pursuit of happiness down the toilet, to where nothing but anarchy was on the horizon.

Well, the soldier didn't have a problem with any talking heads labeling his methods as extreme, unconstitutional and whatever else. America was at war, and Bolan was on the front lines. And there were hundreds, if not thousands more innocents lined up in jihad sights.

Not this day. No more.

Whatever it takes.

As usual, Brognola paved the road to hell in Los Angeles, with Agent Belasko once again in charge of the big Fed's Omega teams. The rest was up to Bolan, and this time the soldier was bent on getting the jump on the enemy. It was pushing noon, and sunny southern California hadn't blown up in a terrorist firestorm.

The Executioner could feel another "not yet" around the corner.

It was his show, his turn to apply the heat and the pain, and he was going to make the best of it—and the worst of it for the opposition.

U-Store-It was planted near the Long Beach Harbor, tucked in among other warehouses. It was surrounded by a chain-link fence, isolated from a smattering of other businesses, watched by security cameras. The property wasn't much in terms of size or numbers of bins. No, it wouldn't take much to wander right past the place on the way to more eye-pleasing waterfront, but apparently it had served its purposes for Jong and his Iraqi company. It was now under Justice Department lock and key. And the FBI and Omega teams were under Bolan's strict orders to not interfere or come knocking on the warehouse door under any circumstances once the private show started.

The Executioner had his motivational speech down, his moves mentally choreographed. The MP-5 was a prop, but if it fell according to intent, the subgun carried his magic bullet. He strode through the entrance, found them sitting well apart at a large worktable, sullen, smoking. They jolted in their chairs and exchanged looks. Bolan reached up and pulled down the roll-away door to the warehouse.

Privacy. Silence.

He took off the mirrored aviator shades, slipped them in a pouch of his combat vest, boring them with the full effect of a no-nonsense measuring. "Get up."

The Iraqi snorted, muttering something in his native tongue.

The Executioner took the clip he'd wedged in his

belt, snapped it in place and hit the bolt. He almost had their attention, Jong looking set to rise, but obviously the Iraqi needed some encouragement. Bolan hit the SMG's trigger, spraying a short burst over their heads. They flinched, one of them yelping as the 9 mm rounds screamed off concrete behind them, whistling off to the shadowy recesses of the warehouse.

They jumped to their feet, the Iraqi cursing.

"Move closer together."

Still reluctant, or defiant. Another burst, aimed just above their heads, and they were dancing toward each other.

"Are you crazy?" Jong bleated. "I have rights. I am a legitimate American citizen."

Bolan let loose another burst, Jong hitting the deck. "Get up or I can leave you there for good."

Jong stood, and Bolan could see he was on the verge of making at least one of them a believer. The Executioner moved forward, edging into their personal space, Jong shaking, backing up a foot or two, but the Iraqi held his ground. Bolan only needed one of them. He would bet Jong was the real information broker between the two, arming the Iraqis, head stuffed with details, since he was Chongjin's boy in L.A. Either way, the Executioner didn't much care who became the example. One of them would talk, or both would live a little while in great pain to regret any stonewalling. In this instance, the soldier had no problem with a cold-blooded execution.

"I'm thinking you're from North Korea," Bolan began. "I'm thinking you're just another Colonel Chongjin stooge, but you know how many and where the Iraqis are. I'm also looking for a man named Bowen," he said, and described his enemy.

Jong pursed his lips, shaking his head, playing dumb. "I know of no such character."

"I'm thinking he's out here looking to get paid while he's jerking my chain. I'm thinking there's some place you know Chongjin maybe has a nice war chest to keep the troops paid and happy. Some business front. And you were caught, sword in hand, so you're finished unless you give up your buddies first."

The Iraqi shook his head. "You can't do this."

"And why's that?"

He chuckled. "Like he said. We have rights. This is America."

"I'll tell you what you have." Bolan stooped, laid the subgun on the floor. "Thirty seconds to start talking. Here's how it works. Just like a quiz show. I ask questions, you give me answers. For every wrong answer," he said, patting the butt of the hip-holstered Desert Eagle, "I blast off a body part. But, any time you want off the show, there's one way out of here." The soldier stepped back. "Through me."

He caught the Iraqi looking at the subgun then to the North Korean, and back to the big man in black.

"Oh, I have your attention now. Good." He glanced at his watch. "Thirty seconds, here we go. I hear you're calling yourself Duahbi. I think your real name is something more like Tarat. As in 'the Rat.' A drowning one. I'll start with you. Your buddies in New York and Chicago are out of the game. They lost. I know, I was there. I gladly did my part to send them on their way to hell."

Bolan turned his side to them, caught the rage building in the Iraqi's eyes, the soldier sensing he'd just turned on the revenge spigot. "I know the North Koreans helped get a bunch of Iraqi murderers of women and children into this country. Your leader thinks he's going to get missiles and guidance systems and all kind of high-tech from Chongjin. Only the colonel probably sees you guys as just cannon fodder, something to use and throw away. How's that make you feel anyway, Rat?"

"You son of a whore!"

"Unarmed, defenseless women and kids. Bunch of heroes. Ten seconds." Bolan pivoted another few inches away from them, nearly painting a bull's-eye on his back, the Iraqi thinking about going for broke. "If you're looking for me to cut you some slack, Rat, well, let's just say I've been blowing away your jihad pals for two days. I got up on the wrong side of the bed and since I haven't slept since I kicked the crap of your jihad buddies in Brooklyn, but you already know that."

He was fast, Bolan gave him that. The Iraqi was a blur in the corner of his eye, the soldier's combat senses feeling the move before it actually happened. Bolan waited long enough, freed the Desert Eagle in a snap fluid draw.

The HK subgun was rising when the Executioner unleashed a roar of steel-jacketed thunder. He aimed high, and the .44 Magnum round blasted through the Iraqi's nose, cleaving off half his skull. He was airborne, body and weapon sailing past Jong. The North Korean watched the corpse slam down. Jong was trembling, wheeling as the Executioner rolled toward him, lifting the massive Desert Eagle.

"Your turn, Jong. I believe I put a question to you."

"Okay, okay!" His arms shot up, hands flapping. "Aloha Productions—that is the only place I know of the colonel would keep what you say."

"Keep talking. And don't make me repeat myself."

Bolan listened as Jong prattled on. He couldn't talk fast enough. A porn factory in North Hollywood, combo stash house and extortion central. It wasn't much, but it was all the soldier had. If Bowen knew of its existence and importance to the operation, he would head there.

Bolan would work out the details with Omega team during the drive.

"What else?"

"What else what?"

Bolan raised the Desert Eagle. "Where are the others like Rat holed up?"

Jong proved he had an amazing memory, apologizing for his earlier lapses, he was under a lot of stress lately. Fourteen—now thirteen Iraqis—were spread around L.A. One house in Long Beach, two apartments, one in Compton, the other in Downey. Had they moved out already? Jong didn't know, he thought so, he couldn't raise them. But Chongjin was supposed to call him, then Jong would place the call to the cell leader, only he guessed the Iraqis were acting on their own.

"Now what?" Jong asked.

Bolan suddenly thought about all the innocent victims he'd left behind in New York, Oklahoma and Chicago, and Jong was only concerned about himself. His blood ran hot, the soldier aware he was sighting down the Desert Eagle, Jong's wide eyes framed.

"I helped you! What is this? You kill me now in cold blood?"

"I can. And I should."

Bolan holstered the weapon.

"So?"

"So, what?"

"I helped you, what is it I get in return?"

The Executioner turned away before he changed his mind. Jong was still ranting, something about a deal, immunity, Witness Protection Program, but Bolan wasn't listening and left the building.

There was a Reaper on the loose to slay.

"I WANT TO ASSURE the three of you that your safety, and the continued well-being of your families, is my primary goal."

They were gathered in the war room. Chongjin stood on the other side of the table, addressing them. He spoke both to inform Shaw, Monroe and Parker of their value to him alive, and to remind the surviving members of the Phoenix Council they would proceed as planned, no matter how afraid, how dangerous or insane they found the bailout phase. The bodies of the slain VIPs, killed by Temple, were left were they fell, one still sitting upright, some brigadier general from the Pentagon, Chongjin believed. The dead were a grim reminder to all of them, he hoped, that no one and nothing would stop him, the face of death warning them the ultimate price for disobedience. Chongjin noted the dead were getting the lion's share of attention, which was both good and bad. He needed to maintain instilling the right of amount of fear across the board, but he didn't want them thinking he would just as soon kill them, too.

Either way, Chongjin didn't have much time to spare for a pep talk. They were well out over the Pacific now, screens clear of hostile aircraft, although Temple had informed him they were monitored by ground radar when they had passed over California. The superplane was now on autopilot, and the major had programmed the bearings into GlobeSpecter's computer, vectoring for a two-hundred-mile passage north of the Hawaiian islands. The rendezvous with the nuclear sub, the *Kim Jong Il,* was a worrisome matter that demanded his attention. The delay in New Mexico had cost them several hours, but Chongjin personally knew the commander of the submarine, and the man wouldn't simply turn around and head back for port. He would lose more than rank if he did that.

"In a short time," Chongjin went on, "perhaps the most perilous moments of our voyage will take place." He caught the men of the council fidgeting, looking at each other, unnerved by the idea of jumping from the plane to the ocean. They thought there must be another way. Why not simply fly the plane all the way to North Korea? And so on. The colonel didn't need to explain himself. The planned rendezvous had been laid out long ago.

"There must be calm when this time comes. Everyone will do as they are told, or the consequence will simply be death. The three of you and your families will remain by my side when this moment comes. I will guide you through it, short of holding your hands."

"But you don't intend to fill us in on this so-called perilous moment," Monroe said.

"Not at this time."

"How long do you think you can hold us hostage in North Korea?" Parker asked.

"As long as it takes. One year, two years, five years. You and your families will be treated as honored guests. You will have all the comforts you are accustomed to in America. You will want for nothing, you will never be in any danger as long as you perform the task we put to you."

"If you're looking to build your own SDI program," Monroe said, "even we were still five to ten years away, maybe more. It will take a lot more than dreaming whatever your master scheme is."

"I am not interested in population defense. My country is not looking to build some mythical laser screen in outer space. We don't plan to shoot down missiles launched at us in the event of an all-out nuclear war, although we will uncover the technology behind your SDI and use it to circumvent your antimissile defense."

"You're looking to advance the offensive," Parker stated.

"Precisely."

"You're insane," Parker said.

"No, we are determined to become the world's foremost nuclear superpower. You know that my country has ICBMs capable of hitting Alaska. We need to fine-tune all of it. An ICBM is generally two or three rockets on top of each other, around a central rocket, as you know. We need to produce smaller, faster and lighter ICBMs. We need to refine the boost phase, where, I understand, it is actually the only real dangerous stage. The ICBM, as you understand, leaving the earth's atmosphere is when one of your magic kill vehicles has any chance of shooting it down. We likewise need to accelerate the postboost phase where a missile slows down, coasting through outer space on its way to reentry. Speed in space, multiple independent reentry warheads perhaps cloaked by solar deflectors in the event your antimissile defense does become fine-tuned in the near future. We have the tools and the technology. We are processing more weapons-grade uranium and plutonium by the week, enough to soon compete in sheer numbers of warheads alone with your country, China and Russia. But we need your expertise. You will be working with our best scientists. Your knowledge will become ours."

"Or else," Parker stated.

"I sincerely hope it doesn't come down to that."

"You must think our military will just sit in the stands, shrug it off as a hopeless international standoff and do nothing to come and get us back?" Monroe asked.

"You're referring, of course, to some covert operation to penetrate my sovereign, peace-loving nation and attempt to free you by force," Chongjin said, smiling. "If that happens, it will prove most unfortunate for all concerned. In that event, your country may have to forget ever tapping any more oil reserves in Alaska."

"You'd launch an ICBM at Alaska just to hold on to us?" Monroe said.

"It would get serious consideration. Of course, both sides would negotiate before such a calamity...but there are other plans inside the one you see before you. Mr. Shaw? Why are we getting no input from you?"

Shaw was silent, staring at the table, then looked up.
"My family, that's my only concern, the only reason I
will continue to cooperate and go along with this mad-
ness. However, should anything happen to them, you
might as well put a bullet in my head yourself."

"I will take that under advisement. Let me be clear
Mr. Shaw, you cannot fight me. There is no way out."

"Oh, I'll fight you if my wife or my daughter is
harmed, even a goddamn scratch or the wrong look
their way from one of your thugs."

"Then I believe we understand each other," Chongjin
told him, wanting to pursue it some more, but Temple
came through on the intercom.

"Colonel."

"That will be all for now, gentlemen," Chongjin said.
Wallace and two other guards moved in to escort them
back to their seats. He went to the intercom box. "Yes,
Major."

"We have contact."

"The submarine?"

"We're in range for their radio transmission. Commander Ohm is trying to patch through as we speak."

"I'm on the way."

Chongjin heard one of the council members clearing his throat. Hill called out to him. He knew what was
coming, his anger building like a rumbling volcano.
"Colonel, hold on! I think we need to finish our previ-
ous discussion."

Chongjin lost it, wheeling on them, and roared,
"There will be no further discussion! We will all do it
or we will all die!"

Chongjin let it sink in for a few seconds, found them

averting his stare, Hill shaking his head, silently telling him he still disagreed.

"Do it or die," Chongjin told them, and swept through the hatch.

THE EXECUTIONER FELT it slipping away again. All of it seemed to be vanishing, like the Iraqi terrorists, before his eyes, and he was likewise beginning to wonder if Bowen had even made it to Los Angeles.

Each stash house Jong had given up had been raided. Empty, all of them, the Iraqis now on the move, but where? The skies over Los Angeles were swarming with police choppers and military gunships, choked with Special Forces commandos who were ready to descend on any jihad movement. Every uniformed patrolmen, SWAT, FBI and Justice agent available was either prowling the streets or spread around L.A. and its suburbs, hunkered and watching studios, airports, every major downtown building that would prove an optimum target. The governor had gone on radio and television at Brognola's insistence, alerting people to the potential of a terrorist attack, but calling for calm, urging all citizens to either remain at home, return there if they could or simply stay put indoors until further notice. Would it be enough?

Bolan peered through the tripod-mounted binoculars. Aloha Productions was roughly a block southwest from the top-floor room of the high-rise apartment Brognola had snapped up for this stakeout. Three special agents on Bolan's Omega One team were now squeezed around the portable police scanners and radio console, monitoring the situation, com-links on.

Waiting for the grim news that jihad had come to Los Angeles.

A watch check, and Bolan felt as if time were standing still. He'd been sitting at the window and watching the front gate to Aloha Productions for over two hours now. One guard at the open gate, clearly armed. Muscle. How many more inside? Palm trees had been planted at staggered intervals in a poor attempt to conceal security cameras mounted on the chain-link fencing. It wasn't as if they could get blueprints on the place from city hall, but the owner was confirmed as Korean. The studio itself hogged an entire block, but only one entrance into the place, Bolan observed, through double doors just beyond the parking lot. Mostly luxury vehicles down there, a dozen or so having cleared out. All faces, coming or going, were noted by Bolan.

No sign of Bowen.

Okay, he thought, figure the day's shoots were wrapping up, the sun ready to go down. Which meant evening rush hour. Maybe that's what the enemy was waiting for, he feared. A mass exodus, more crowds, restaurants packed, traffic bottlenecks on the freeways.

Bolan watched a man and woman pile into a Mercedes and head out for the gate. Omega units and the FBI had that side covered, ready to raise Agent Belasko the second Bowen appeared. For their part, Bolan had briefed all agents on procedure and tactics once—if—Bowen showed up.

A straight charge inside, take it down, teams assigned their roles, with Bolan leading the rush. Snipers had been positioned on the roof of the high-rise. If they were armed inside and showed even a nanosecond of hostile intent, the standing order was to shoot to kill. No exceptions.

Shadows began stretching over the white stucco building. Forty-six minutes dragged.

Bolan looked over at his Omega agents. "Anything?"

A shake of the head from Agent Wilkinson. Too quiet out there in the city. Bolan felt his gut telling him it was going to happen.

Where was Bowen? he wondered. Maybe he had already come and gone. Bolan discarded the thought as soon it formed. It wasn't Bowen's style to make a quiet exit. The man had left his message in Chicago, clearly craving an L.A. showdown. By doing that, Bowen would have to figure his nemesis would somehow pick up the trail. The soldier was thinking it was about more money for Bowen, too, no telling how much illicit cash was inside the porn factory. Greed and bloodlust, after all, were kissing cousins, he knew. If Bowen had already paid a visit there, he would have made some noise, probably leaving behind another message, bodies everywhere, uniforms storming the place by now.

The soldier was considering paying the porn producers a personal visit, shake the nest up, when the black Towncar slid in to the gate. The driver's window came down, a Korean face framed in Bolan's telescopic sights as he adjusted to the distance.

"Heads up," Bolan told his agents. The muscle was at the window, peering into the back, body language telling Bolan they were expected but the guard at the gate didn't like it. The Towncar drove on, parked. Bolan felt his blood race, doors opening—

Bowen stepped out.

The Executioner had the tac radio in hand, bolting out of his chair. He patched through on the frequency to all units. "He's here. I'm on the way down. I want everybody one block west on Sherman, but sit tight. Copy?"

Confirmed, and Bolan snatched up his M-16/M-203 combo, flying for the door. It was time to drop the curtain on the man's Hollywood act before it got started, the Executioner determined.

End of show, no encore.

Shoot to kill.

14

"I was becoming concerned, Colonel. I was afraid some unfortunate incident had occurred while you were in America."

"A minor delay, Commander." Chongjin looked at his handheld GPS module, tapping in their present position, activating their tracking monitor. "Are you receiving our signal, Commander?"

"Yes."

"Major?"

Chongjin watched as Temple's fingers flew over the keyboard of the computer. The major was hunched in the navigational workstation, numbers scrolling so fast across the monitor it was all a white blur to Chongjin. Temple checked and double-checked all screens on the instrument panel for various readings. All of it was state-of-the-art, with digital readouts, and the major had briefly boasted about the cutting-edge magic of the navigation computers, leaving Chongjin wondering whose benefit—or regret—the lecture was meant for. There was a computer that calculated all bearings at lightning speed, charting any course needed, practically on its own, or so the major had stated. There was even wind scale, with a voice-activated weather report, down to temperature readings of the ocean's surface. There was a device that measured the strength of the sea's chop, tides and currents. There was aneroid barometer, advanced Doppler radar, Ageton tables and so on, just to name a few items that left Chongjin impressed with this display of Western genius. It was a shame, he thought, but he was sinking this ship soon. Another gesture of defiance, another way to dig the knife deeper into those he believed had too much of an edge in technology, controlled far too much of the world's affairs.

Another statement.

"With the sub's present position and depth, and our present weight on board, plus calculating speed and distance, before and after I cut the engines, I can start dropping us from our current twenty thousand feet down to five thousand and cut the engines there like you want. Call it six miles of sailing from there until it crashes. Any closer and I run the risk of landing her right on top of your sub. This much weight it would take that perfect storm to knock us off-course, so I'm not worried about her when she's left on her own. Tell Commander Ohm he'll need to start for the surface in fifty-three minutes. Our DZ will end up—well, factor in the winds at a thousand feet for the jump at eighteen to twenty miles per hour—approximately four miles and change due southeast from where he surfaces. Let me give you the exact heading for pickup. Oh, and Colonel? Feel free to converse in English. You can't trust me at this late stage, you and me got a serious problem."

Chongjin balked, but put on his smile. "You will have to excuse Commander Ohm, Major. His English is limited."

"Whatever. Here it is."

And Chongjin relayed the numbers. Commander Ohm copied, and Chongjin said, "Until we meet on board, Commander. Over and out."

Chongjin studied Temple's dark expression, something inside deflating the man. "Your wonder computer tells you all of that?"

"Let me put it this way, Colonel. The computers the NSA uses are Smith-Corona typewriters compared to what I've got here."

"If I'm not mistaken, Major, you almost sound as if you regret what we are about to do."

"Trashing this prototype doesn't exactly make my day, Colonel. You mind me asking exactly why you want to sink this craft to the bottom of the ocean?"

"I intend to do more than sink it, Major. Once I jump, I will blow it to scrap right before it hits the water."

"Again, why?"

"Because I can."

"Another middle-finger salute, Colonel? If you can't have it, nobody can."

"Who says I couldn't have it if I wanted it?"

"I guess I just don't understand that kind of thinking. It's all a sorry waste, if you ask me."

"Do your job. You aren't going to be paid five million dollars, Major, for your memoirs of this voyage."

The hard edge returned to Temple's voice. "Just make sure I do get paid, and soon, Colonel."

Chongjin felt his smile stretch.

Temple turned back to his monitors. "If that's all, Colonel, I've got some last-minute touching-up to do. And, according to the computer's math, you've got about sixty-three minutes to get those passengers through jump school."

Chongjin forced himself to delay the inevitable. He still needed the major, but...

"Call me as soon as you cut the engines, Major. Do you hear me?"

"I heard. Just make sure you have a parachute ready for me, Colonel—but one with a red tag on the bottom right hand corner. You know, the same ones you'll be handing out to Shaw, Monroe and all that precious human cargo of yours."

Insolent bastard, Chongjin thought, losing the smile, then forced himself to leave the flight deck.

BOWEN COULD FEEL the home stretch, but he wasn't counting money or about to chuckle yet. The day so far had his nerves jumping around like firecrackers. Delays everywhere. First, their airfield was way the hell up past Barstow. Then it took some haggling over the pilot's role, the flight jockey not sure he wanted to stick around until Bowen finally parted with a ten-grand advance, about all the cash he had on him. Then traffic was a mess just getting into Los Angeles. One of the Koreans pulled out the police scanner—and where the hell had that been?—and they navigated around roadblocks, checkpoints and aerial sweeps. The alert had been sounded over the radio, cops everywhere, their City of Angels just short of the equal to the military's Threat-

Con Delta, maybe martial law around the bend. Bowen found himself suddenly pulling for the Iraqis to get to work and soon. Cover his withdrawal, at least, when this was a wrap, fat cash bulging out the nylon bag.

Well, he was in and on his way now, the Koreans leading the tour. Hello, Aloha Productions, he thought, screw the gorilla at the gate with his silk suit and dirty looks. The call had been placed ahead of time, Bu-Jin expecting present company, didn't sound happy about it, so Bowen was braced for attitude, and then some. No firm details for Bu-Jin over the phone, just be there, Bowen making sure the whole conversation was in English and not their machine-gun sushi gibberish.

"Nice and easy, girls," Bowen warned the North Koreans, the Desert Eagle out and low by his leg. "It's almost over, all but the laughing and the counting of Benjamin crispies."

They were strolling along down a thickly carpeted, wide catwalk that overlooked all the fun and games, the walls adorned with posters of some of Aloha Productions finer works of art, he reckoned. Skip the skin presentations, the titles alone inflamed his imagination. There was...well, forget the fan adulation, Bowen grinned down at what they considered hard labor here. The running glass partition was soundproof, floor to ceiling. He couldn't hear the first grunt or moan considering all the activity he found under way. It was a pit of silent lust down there, Bowen wondering what time the tour guide started, as if the place were Paramount or Burbank Studio, bring grandma and the kids. Each set stood alone, sectioned off by ten-foot wall, all of it forming an arena. They didn't keep banker's hours, he gave them that, most of the cameras still rolling that late in the day. Sleazy-looking types all over the pit, he thought, directors most likely, soundlessly barking out orders. There was a Southern plantation, poolside cabana, a locker room with cheerleaders acting out every jock's fantasy at the moment. A scaled-down mock-up of a cruise ship. Kitchens and bedrooms. A torture chamber where some leggy blonde in full black leather regalia was whipping the tar out of some poor bastard, that guy, Bowen thought, most definitely earning his paycheck.

"Who loves ya, buddy?" Bowen said, laughing.

It was a rainbow of skin all over the place, Bowen observed, mostly Asian girls, but a scattering of Americans. Bu-Jin was an equal-opportunity employer, a real swell guy, he could be sure. Every conceivable sex act, natural or otherwise, Bowen found, lesbian gigs, toys galore, full-blown orgies, some stagehands off to the side huffing up blow...

"Welcome to Hollywood," Bowen said. "You know, ladies, when the smoke of this mess clears, all the hard feelings die down and life is beautiful all around again, I might see if I can buy myself in on a cut of this action. I always saw myself landing somehow in show biz. Yeah, this is definitely my style, the way to go. Girls, girls, girls. I know, you didn't think I had this sensitive side. What can I say? I'm an art lover."

Bowen came alert, rounding the bend. There were two of them and it wasn't hard to tell who was what. Another guard, clearly packing, and a short Korean in ponytail, rolling for the intercept.

"Mr. Bu-Jingles, I presume?" Bowen said.

"What is the meaning of this? Who are you? The colonel didn't mention anything about this visit! And...what did you call me?"

Bowen got the show started. He launched one of the Koreans into Bu-Jin. They were tangled up, grappling to pull themselves apart when Bowen thrust the Desert Eagle at the guard's face.

"I called you a scumbag sushi asshole is what! Anybody moves, I even hear a deep breath, I start blasting. Turn around," he told the guard. A look over his shoulder, the other Korean frozen in place, and Bowen brought the barrel down, brained the guard. A ton of thunder hit the deck, Bowen swinging his aim, stepping up, muzzle pressed between the porn producer's eyes.

"Where's the cash?"

"You are..."

"I know, I know, I'm making a big mistake."

"I have almost twenty armed security men inside this building."

Bowen bared his teeth at one of the Koreans. "You little fucks neglected to mention the place was an armed camp."

"You never asked."

Bowen chuckled. Oh, but that guy was priceless, damn near his kind of guy. He would be sure to save a bullet for the smart-ass. "The money. Two seconds. One..."

"In my office."

"Kimmy, shake a leg, get up here, in front." Bowen waited, stepped back. A quick search of the catwalk. Clear. And they were too busy down in love-land, he glanced, to bother with his strong-arm gig. "Turn around, everybody start walking. Real easy. Just like a public tour. Oh, and by the way, Bu-Jin? Any goons want in on the act, anybody waiting behind door number one to your office, you can kiss goodbye that part of you makes it all go round here."

"There is no one in my office."

"Sounds like heaven."

"LISTEN TO ME very carefully, people. I will only go through this one time."

Before Chongjin launched into his spiel, Wallace made a show of scanning the crowd, the colonel glancing his way while he eased a few steps nearer to the first of two bins. The colonel, holding up the demonstration pack, caught him looking into the bin, shot him another glimpse then back to the crowd.

This was not going to be good, Wallace knew. Hell, it was going to be a disaster.

Snafu.

Wallace, his immediate people, the other guards and the council had already been briefed on the jump. The big shots voiced all kinds of objections, squawking for another option to bypass the header for the Pacific. Why jump? Why destroy an aircraft that could prove a gold mine of technology for the colonel's side? Why...well, Chongjin, he knew, had somehow beaten down the urge to start blasting away right there in the war room, which told Wallace the colonel still needed all hands, top to bottom on the pecking order. Plus, as the colonel pointed out, he was jumping with them— what's the problem?—as if that answered all questions, fears to rest, the whole scheme supposed to make sense now since he was going out the door right along with them. The ex-DIA, NSA and FEMA men were scared to jump, and since they'd probably never done it, he could understand the fear. Having done a stint as an Army Ranger, he knew a little something about this aspect of the operation. When he was first informed about this part of the voyage, though, Wallace had wondered what genius had conjured up this mess. Of course, it had been Chongjin, and Wallace had almost withdrawn his services from the council, only by then he was too far along in the planning phase. Then there was the money.

He flickered his gaze over the lake of faces, then noted the red tab on the bottom of the pack Chongjin displayed. That meant one of two things. Either the rigger had done some sloppy packing for bin number two, or packs were minus canopies altogether, maybe the rip cord proving to be just that—ripping away. When they jumped, Wallace pictured 101 things going wrong to endanger all their lives. He could see a number of them freezing up in midair, could probably single out the free-fall statues if he searched their faces long enough, but why bother. From a thousand feet up, it was analogous to jumping from the Golden Gate Bridge, times four. Anyone with a canopy malfunction, or no canopy at all, would hit the water like a swan dive from a tall building to sidewalk. Then there were rip-cord pull problems, and it wasn't as easy, he knew, as they made it look on TV. He could already envision collisions on the way down if these amateurs—and he couldn't even classify them as that—didn't work the steering lines. Then there was landing in the water itself. Get tangled up in the steering line, risers, canopy. Didn't unbuckle the harness belts fast enough. Shadows of the others churning in the water for the surface, turning on the mass panic, with people seeing man-eating sharks where it was only the guy thrashing next to them.

He might question the colonel's sanity at this point, but Wallace would make damn sure he got his hands on packs with red tabs, the same ones as the SDI trio and family.

"This aircraft is going to crash into the ocean," Chongjin said, and the reaction was predictable. He shouted for silence and continued on. "But this is your lifeline. This is a parachute. Now, pay attention! I will give you a full and complete demonstration."

Dead silence fell over the hostages.

"I can see I have everyone's undivided attention. Good."

No shit, Wallace thought, and listened as Chongjin pointed to the steel clasp and the rip cord. He started off by assuring them all these parachutes were designed specifically for this moment of their journey, his own hands having assisted in the rigging. He called them idiot-proof.

It was all Wallace could do to stifle the groan.

BOWEN KNEW he wasn't overreacting when he sensed it was all about to unravel. It felt too easy. So far nobody coming, nobody waiting, either, in the office suite. He never trusted somebody who might be telling the truth.

"If I see anything but money come out of the safe, Bu-Jin, you're fired!"

He checked his two Koreans, both of them laid out, facedown. They were nearly sunken an inch or so in the carpet, but managed to look up and show him some fire in the eyes. The office suite itself would have been something to admire under different circumstances, Bowen thought. Hot tub and sauna, minigym, a bar the area of a basketball court. But the bank of cameras hanging above Bu-Jin's car-sized desk was about all Bowen cared to watch. The monitors looked to cover the lot, the only outside doors into the porn palace, the hall leading to the office, then, of course, eyes peeping in on the money-making machine in the pit.

The vault was open, Bowen thinking he could whiff fresh ink on new bills. "Back up! Eat some carpet! Do it!" he roared at the porn king, bounding up to the landing where the guy's desk sat like his personal altar.

Bowen went to work with savage haste. The MP-5 was out, spare clips going into his waistband, a few frag grenades dumped into the trench coat. He tried to control his breathing, but he was too excited, with paranoia and fear rising as he kept whipping his head around, making sure everybody was staying put, cameras clear of party crashers. No time to count his take, but he shoved dozens of rubber-banded stacks of hundreds, swelling the bag in seconds.

"I'm in heaven," he started to sing. He had the safe cleaned out, then glanced up the cameras and—

The party was over.

It was a blur, head spinning, ears roaring, his heart derailing. Impossible to take all the commotion in at once, but he counted four of them with subguns, hitting the front entrance doors. Belasko was in the lead, assault rifle with attached grenade launcher. Another day, he would have laughed, eager for the showdown.

But this was payday, and he had dreams to live out, paradise to see.

Belasko, though, was a face he'd see in his nightmares, framed in the camera eye, there then gone. Any other time...

The one-man wrecking crew next proved the least of his problems.

There were men on the run, charging, weapons out.

Something came flying for his blind side next. Bowen whipped around, Desert Eagle up. He tapped the trigger, putting one .44 Magnum round in the Korean's chest and sent him flying.

15

The porn men wasted no time trying to save the palace. The security camera was nearly invisible to the naked eye, but Bolan spotted the glass bubble above the jamb, figured—then sensed on combat adrenaline—they were on the way. The opposition proved they weren't coming to hand out tickets for the tour guide. A few rounds sprayed the door, pistols barking, a burst of autofire. But Bolan was already in, rocking on and tapping the M-203's trigger, missile on the way, as Omega team's subgun storm caused the hardmen to lurch, duck and throw their aim wide.

The soldier's thunderous 40 mm entrance cleared the path to take the foyer, sending men flying like tenpins. It looked like a straight run now up the ramp, leading out into what he believed was the belly of the studio.

Show time.

There was a glass wall at the end of ramp, obscured now by smoke from the frag blast, he saw. Corners, he knew. And shooters could be heading from both directions.

Three down. How many hardmen left who would

fight to save the sleaze empire? One way to find out, and Bolan wasn't about to bail Aloha Productions, dissatisfied with the tour.

Too close now, he could almost feel Bowen nearby. Call it justice, vengeance, whatever, but the Executioner wanted to tag the bastard himself.

No mercy, no chance in hell for that guy.

As the first one through the door, Bolan stuck close to the foyer wall, on the charge up, listening for pounding feet, voices somewhere flying high up the panic meter. Omega One on his heels, the Executioner made the far edge of the wall, peered around the corner in both ways down the closed-off catwalk, his assault rifle searching for fresh targets. The autofire ripped open on his right flank. He snatched an eyeful of three more skinflick thugs on the prowl and flung himself out of the line of fire, just as rounds sliced off the corner edge. Bolan plucked a frag bomb from his webbing, armed it as Omega One fell in behind. A low underhand pitch of the steel egg, around the corner.

And somebody screamed to clear out.

The thunderclap answered their fear and panic.

With no recon, no clue really about the interior layout, Bolan took it in as best he could. The catwalk, like a running track in a gym, looked to circle above an arena where Aloha Productions rolled the cameras, sweetening, no doubt in his mind, the terror pot. The masses down there, some clothed, some naked and some grabbing up whatever they could find in haste, were staring up, bouncing off each other, human pinballs. The smarter ones were already in exodus. Just what he needed now, the soldier thought, civilians, the innocent—or not so innocent—maybe getting tangled up in the line of fire. Then there was Bowen, somewhere in the building, and the man had shown he didn't much give a damn about collateral damage. If Bowen was cornered, the soldier could expect to deal with a human shield or two.

A look at the dead strewed at his feet, the Executioner made out enough of their features where shrapnel hadn't diced them up into ground beef.

Korean.

A Chongjin operation, a porn distribution center to help finance the enemy's whole bloody conspiracy. The Executioner intended to burn it down. There was no other way.

Bowen first.

Then Bolan made out the echoing ring of gunfire. A big weapon, cannonfire pealing far down the walk, around the bend. Voices were raised in alarm from that direction. Whatever the bloody sideshow, smart money told Bolan that Bowen was in fighting withdrawal and bailing.

The Executioner relayed the orders down the line, put Agent Harley in charge of the unit. Within moments, the FBI would come running, locking into firefights wherever the porn thugs stood their turf.

Bolan took Agent Michaels to watch his back, and set off to hunt Bowen.

"LIGHTS, BABY!"

Bowen hit the other Korean with blast number two, a head shot that redecorated a white leather couch with brains and muck and chunks of skull, dumping him to the carpet at the end of the ungainly rocket ride.

"Camera, assholes!"

Two Korean shooters nearly made it through the doors, subguns chattering, crazed by panic and false hope. But Bowen knew they were coming already, had them nailed with two rounds to the chest before they could adjust their aim. He laughed at the sight of them flung back into the hall, skidding on their butts, out of sight, out of mind.

He did a one-eighty on his heels and lined up the colonel's man in L.A. Bu-Jin looked set to beg for his life, hands up, the man shaking as though afflicted by some nervous disorder.

Why was it, he briefly wondered, they all played with fire, but when it came time to pony up to the Reaper they thought they could plead and bargain for their lives?

"Don't!"

"Action!"

Bowen blew him away, a point-blank chest shot that picked him up, hurled him into the wall. He looked pinned there for a heartbeat, a mashed insect for dissection, then slid into a boneless pile, trailing a greasy smear.

"I always wanted to say that. Goddamn, but I love show biz!"

Bowen stowed the Desert Eagle. Grabbing the HK subgun, the Reaper geared up for numbers. Bring them on. He scanned the cameras. A small army of helmeted and armored FBI shooters was running across the lot to make the big show. Backup. No sign of Belasko on the monitors, but he was somewhere—that much Bowen knew. Right then, the Reaper found he had six very pissed-off Koreans hunkered outside the office. They were jabbering away, cradling subguns, flapping hands at the doors.

Bowen knew what was coming.

Mass charge, rush in and start shooting up the place, a whole lot of spray and pray.

No sweat.

They'd better start praying, he thought.

Some dark rage began to settle over him. All hope wasn't lost yet, but he could feel time, and luck, running out. He couldn't go back the way he'd come, not without slamming into Belasko. Looked like payday for everybody. Cash for him, bullets for any chump who stood in his way.

Bowen slipped the booty bag around his shoulder, eyes on the Koreans in the hall, the pack hesitating still, gathering their courage, no doubt, looked as if no one really wanted to be the first one through the door.

"Fuck 'em," Bowen said, took a frag grenade, pulled the pin.

The Reaper bounded off the landing, pitched the steel baseball just as they came running.

CHONGJIN COULD DO his own math, and he didn't need any computer to tally the score. He had the paces to the flight deck mentally marked off, had clocked them, too, when he'd left the major to his wonder toys and to shut down the GlobeSpecter.

Everything was set for the jump, nothing left to do but free-fall for ocean and wait for pickup. His human cargo was all harnessed into their parachutes, herded now into the loading bay, Wallace standing by. They were in a good degree of panic back there, but Chongjin knew his point was made. They could stay if they liked and go down with the plane or jump. Not much of a choice. Everybody was jumping.

Except Temple.

The engines had just been cut. Two minutes and change. It wasn't the easy ride or even close to the smooth sailing Chongjin had expected. The unmanned giant bird was lurching up and down, the walls rumbling as if the damn thing were being kicked around. Whether it was turbulence or the weight of the craft he didn't know.

Whatever it was, the plane was falling like a rock, listing forward.

How much time before it plunged through the ocean surface?

A few minutes left, if he was lucky.

Chongjin, pistol in hand, buckled into his harness and was through the hatch to the war room. He was clearing the door at the same time Temple swept through the opposite hatch. It was perfect timing, Chongjin considered, the intercept saving him a few precious steps.

And seconds to get back and gone from the doomed bird.

The major froze. It was only a heartbeat, two at the most, but realization turned to raw fury in Temple's eyes as Chongjin lifted the pistol.

Temple grabbed for his weapon. "Why, you rotten little—"

Chongjin shot him between the eyes. He had just saved the council five million dollars they really didn't have to spare. But it was also personal, Chongjin knew. He didn't tolerate insolence.

He snatched up the hand-held radio and raised Wallace. "Mr. Wallace, lower the ramp."

THE BLAST WAS a beauty, dead center and kicking them out, all to hell. It appeared to Bowen a home run at first look, bases cleared, then he heard the bleating cries of wounded beyond the cloud. He made out the squirming red mass, two of them clawing the wall like wounded animals on the other side of the hall, crimson bags shrouded by smoke. Walking on, the Reaper held back on the subgun's trigger, ripping them to bloody shreds.

All done.

Time to quit the party.

Past the dead, he took in the bedlam at the far end of the hall, all shouts, screams and the distant snarling of weapons fire from where he'd come. He didn't know the layout of the sprawling studio, what exits he hoped to find, but if he made it below, into the arena, he had to believe there was another way to bail. A trio of naked Asian beauties nearly bowled him over as he rounded the corner. He grabbed one of them by the arm, jerking her back.

"How do I get downstairs, honey?"

She tried to wrench herself free, wild-eyed with terror. Bowen slapped some sense into her.

"Answer me!"

She threw her head over her shoulder. "That door!"

"Is there an exit downstairs!"

"In the back, through the dressing rooms."

Snippy but tough, he thought. He decided to let her live. What the hell, she'd just be some other poor guy's future problem.

Time to pick up the pace and clear out.

He was about to shove her away when Belasko turned up in the corner of his eye, a ghost drifting through the running mass of naked and seminaked flesh. Out of nowhere. She was screaming next, as Bowen locked an arm around her throat, sweeping a long burst around Belasko, but the guy seemed to have jackpot luck. He dropped behind a statue, Bowen hurling his shield away, cursing as his bullets did little more than chip away stone.

The Reaper bolted for the door at the end of the cross-running hall. He whirled, knowing the guy was relentless as a rabid wolf, then triggered off a fusillade at the corner. A little adjustment, he might have nailed the guy—damn it—but his nemesis was ducking back.

Squeezing off another burst, Bowen backpedaled and bulled through the door. A cry of alarm lancing his ears, and he found he hammered through some dude in bikini briefs, a windmill of arms and legs tumbling down the steps on his descent.

"GO!"

Most of them stood, frozen at the edge, heads nodding, eyes wide, as if waiting for somebody else to start the jump. Chongjin blocked off Shaw and family, Monroe and Parker and wives, forcing them all to wait for the others to go. They were losing altitude fast, nothing but blue sky now, the ocean gone from sight, with clouded heavens coming up. The way Chongjin had it figured, the ones who jumped last would end up closest to the submarine for pickup. He wasn't concerned about headings, a few minutes lost, a mile either way, when they hit the water. He was set to send up the biggest flare in history.

"Jump!" Chongjin screamed.

And he started triggering the pistol, firing rounds over their heads. The first batch went, leaping off the edge, couldn't go fast enough as rounds snapped over them, skyward. Chongjin blasted on until the clip burned out, the rest fully motivated now, shoving and slamming into each other before they tumbled out of sight.

"Move it up!" the colonel ordered Shaw and family.

The walls shuddered, floor listing, going up to stern quick, forcing them all to clamber up the ramp. The council, he saw, was next in line. Hill was scowling back, teeth bared. It was all Chongjin could do to keep from pumping one into that expression, but they hurled themselves off the edge.

The blacksuited guards had no problem going airborne; most of them, the colonel knew, were military, experienced jumpers. Wallace was hesitating, scanning faces, looking to Chongjin as if he was about to issue some warning, then flung himself toward the open sky.

"We're next!" Chongjin told Shaw.

THE STAMPEDE WAS thinning out when Bowen made the torture chamber set. Turning, he loosed a burst of SMG fire just as his adversary moved into the door. The guy was quick as lightning, Bowen's rounds sailing past.

No score.

"Son of a bitch."

To add more bloody confusion to the chaos, he tagged a couple of runners heading Belasko's way. The Reaper had them sliced and sailing, retreating through the opening between the wallboards of two sets. The big commando was surging out now, eyes fired up for the kill, but he was forced to sidestep the flying dominoes. Bowen triggered another hasty burst, but his rounds only chopped the last of the fliers.

Bowen seized cover behind the wall. Only one way through all the tables, beds, fake palm trees and whatever else in the chamber or the beachfront set, he figured. Straight ahead for Belasko, a gauntlet of props dictating his course.

He palmed a frag bomb. The pin was out, then gaping holes started falling over his head. Plaster and dust nearly choked him out.

The man was going for broke, blowing up the flimsy wallboard with his hellstorm, raking the works. Bullets snapping over his head as Bowen hit the deck.

Bowen counted off two ticks, and slung his arm around the corner, let the egg fly.

Nothing to do now, the Reaper held on, riding out the storm.

Hoping.

"YOU WILL BE FINE!" Chongjin shouted, his SDI cargo and family fighting the incline to take the edge. "Just pull that ring hard! Take it now in your hands! Jump!"

The girl screamed but sailed away, Shaw and wife airborne next. Chongjin saw Monroe freeze, blubbering something, then he shoved the man out. Three left, Parker, wife and Monroe's woman, and Chongjin bellowed in their ear. It proved plenty enough motivation to send them over the edge.

Then the colonel flew, free-falling, ready for this moment. He twisted his body, jerking himself sideways by the legs and shoulders, and palmed the box. Thumb down on the button, he made his statement.

THE STAGE PROPS FORCED Bolan to fire the M-16 higher than he wanted. Rack table, bed, two cameras in the line of fire, but the Executioner tried to work around them, raking the storm, up and down. He knew Bowen had taken a nosedive, going low, saved maybe for the moment until the soldier could cut the gap, unload point-blank. If that didn't work, a 40 mm grenade was down the chute of the M-203.

He'd take Bowen however he could.

The Executioner had a fresh clip rammed and racked, striding on, his wave of 5.56 mm rounds eating up the painted vegetation, beach scenery blasted all to hell. He was angling away from the torture chamber, lowering the autofire, clear of props, when it came around the corner.

Grenade.

And he could be certain the man had ticked off the numbers. Bowen was insane, he knew, but he was still a pro.

The Executioner scrambled to clear out from the bouncing lethal egg, legs churning. Bolan was flying for cover when the blast shattered his senses.

A couple extra ticks of the clock and fast feet saved

Bolan from being flayed to raw burger by the frag blast. A bolt to the side, launching himself up a short ramp beside a stretching rack, what looked the sturdiest buffer in the torture chamber set, and the Executioner was airborne as the egg blew. Sailing on, the lethal cloud of steel wasps racing after him, Bolan flipped over the edge of a massive bed. Bolan's head bounced off floor, light and noise clouding his brain. The thunderclap crashed, a brick wall of heat and hellish sound. Hard for the soldier to say what happened next, but somehow he reckoned the bed sponged up most of the fire and steel.

And his hands, he found, were empty of the M-16/M-203 combo. Where the—?

No time.

The sound of weapons fire rattled around inside his skull, combat reflex taking over as Bolan dug out the .44 Magnum Desert Eagle. Adrenaline searing away some of the cobwebs, Bolan spotted a tall shadow in black leather trench coat. Face gray as the boiling smoke, dead ahead, he was sweeping the HK MP-5 back and forth, pouring on the 9 mm storm at the soldier's Omega team backup.

Bowen on the move, war bag around his shoulder, locked in and trading fire with the Justice agents. The Executioner gave his adversary all of one microsecond of angry reflection.

Bolan lifted the Desert Eagle, rising, drew a bead. The monster was his to slay, only Bolan's enemy would never know what hit him. Either Bowen figured his frag bomb had done the job, stepping out to confirm his kill, or the man was too caught up concentrating his spray of SMG fire at the agents crouched in the door. Bowen was spinning, by now sensing the deadly problem to his side, no doubt, dropping for dicey cover behind the rack table ruins. He was snarling out the rage, pinned now between the Omega team and the Executioner, his eyes two points of fire, the guy aware now he was history.

Stuck and screwed.

Bolan squeezed the trigger over and over, the .44 Magnum hollowpoint rounds blasting off the chipped teeth of Bowen's rack table shield. The Reaper was still howling out the curses, jerking upright next as the Omega agents sliced him up with subgun fire, driving him into a clear field for Bolan to take out with an easy tag. The black bag came apart from the hail of lead when it slipped down from his shoulder, falling around in front of his chest. Bolan fired on, the booty bag erupting a money rain through the air, red bits and pieces fluttering around Bowen as he danced back, punched this way and that by converging lead hammers. He was eviscerated by Bolan's next round, his HK subgun way off track now, but chattering out his swan song. One more .44 Magnum cannon shot and Bolan nailed his adversary in the chest. Bowen flew back on a showering dissection of guts, blood and leather strands before he slammed into the hull of the cruise ship mock-up.

All done for Bolan's devil in human skin.

The Executioner focused on the battle above. On the move he holstered the mammoth Desert Eagle, scooped up the M-16. More Omega agents had already stormed the porn studio, firefights now raging all over the place. The circular catwalk overlooking the arena of various stage sets appeared to be where most of the engagements were under way. Two Koreans were running behind the glass wall up top, wheeling and triggering Ingram MAC-10s. They were hammering the partition next, greasy crimson smears rolling down the glass before they were lost to Bolan's sight.

Leading two other Omega troops, Agent Michaels was on the tac radio, Bolan hearing the Justice man confirming the report. "We're on the way."

Bolan heard the autofire, men shouting in Korean from some point to the east, hidden from sight by the various scenery walls that made the whole studio a maze of sets and props, shooters perhaps lurking or making a final stand behind every conceivable point of cover.

The soldier heard the problem, three Omega agents at the locker room set, bogged down and trading fire with four porn goons. Bolan gave the Reaper one last look. Three thousand miles, hunting the murderous bastard. How many, good or bad, had he killed? No matter now, it was a major score, nailing a monster that had kept the hydra breathing. But he was only one tentacle. Before long, the Executioner intended to slay the whole beast.

Right now, he had a few good men in trouble.

"Let's roll," Bolan told his three-man Omega team, and led the charge, bent on turning the tide there, make short work of a few more monsters.

Then the North Korean colonel, on deck. Even if he had to infiltrate the colonel's own country...

First the butcher's work there, Chongjin on hold,

but not for long, his life numbered in hours if the Executioner had anything to do with it.

One battle, Bolan told himself, one monster at a time.

*****

Don't miss the exciting conclusion of
THE DOOMSDAY TRILOGY
Look for
ARMAGEDDON EXIT
on sale September 2002.

Take
2 explosive books
plus a
mystery bonus
FREE

James Axler
Outlanders®

FAR EMPIRE

Waging a covert war that ranges from a subterranean complex in the desert to a forgotten colony on the moon, former magistrate Kane, brother-in-arms Grant and archivist-turned-warrior Brigid Baptiste find themselves pawns in a stunning strategy of evil. A beautiful hybrid carries an unborn child—a blueprint for hope in a dark world. She seeks Kane's help, unwittingly leading them into a trap from which there may be no escape....

In the Outlands, the shocking truth is humanity's last hope.